I0633455

Female barbers attached to a pair of scissors that won't stop, women who can't conceal hard-earned wads of hundred dollar bills sticking up from under their polka dot bikini bottoms, gigantic victims and midget killers, sons going mad from killing their mothers, men pushing aimlessly huge wardrobes in empty rooms while contemplating suicide, iconic authors dreaming of being wild asses, Dostoyevskyan virgin prostitutes, men who forget themselves, hen-like spinsters giving birth to pesky pecking roosters, compulsive seductresses who delight in torturing tall wimpy men, all shown in a blinding-bright light on an absurdist stage. Are crocodiles capable of smiling if they can't cry?

ADVANCED PRAISE FOR *CROCODILE SMILES*

In case you have missed the voice of the rich, courageous, adventurous fiction writing of Yuriy Tarnawsky, this collection will be a great introduction. You will experience his unique ability to meld wicked humor and looming gravitas. One of the great under-recognized talents in the fiction of the 20th - 21st century.

—Steve Katz

If Frankenstein had had the wit of Groucho Marx and the painterly subtlety of Magritte he might have written these magical and dangerous stories instead of Yuriy Tarnawsky. The master of short tails has struck again! Frightening, funny and baffling as ever!

—Alain Arias-Misson

Yuriy Tarnawsky's fictional world is one in which every object and every action is meaningful. Haircuts have meaning. Two refrigerators are alive with ominous activity. Kafka meets Sartre (implying hell is... other bugs!). Sweet porridge can "assuage the victim's suffering." The stories are perfectly envisioned, as if Tarnawsky had just landed on this earth with his sense of wonder still intact, looking at everything and trying to understand. Reading these stories is like learning to see all over again!

—Eckhard Gerdes

CROCODILE SMILES

short shrift fictions

YURIY TARNAWSKY

JEF Books

2020

Crocodile Smiles

by Yuriy Tarnawsky

Copyright © 2020 by Yuriy Tarnawsky
Second, Expanded Edition, published as *JEF* 88

ACKNOWLEDGEMENTS

First published as *Crocodile Smiles/short shrift fictions*,
Black Scat Books, 2014.

"The Haircut" first published in *Black Scat Review* No. 4, 2013.
"Dead Darling" first published in *Black Scat Review* No. 1, 2012,
reprinted with minor changes from *Best European Fiction 2014*,
Dalkey Archive Press, 2013.
"On Kicking the Bucket" first published in *Modus Tollens,*
Jaded Ibis Press, 2013.
"Kaffka's Dream" first published in *Black Scat Review* No. 11, 2015.

All of the pieces from the first edition—"The Haircut," "Dead Darling,"
"Agamemnon Post Mortem," "The Revenge," "Insect People," and
"Clara not Schumann but Fick"—reprinted here with minor changes.

ISBN 1-884097-88-X
ISBN-13 978-1-884097-88-1
ISSN 1084-547X

Cover art & design by Norman Conquest
Back cover photograph of the author by Oleh Holovackiy

JEF Books/ Depth Charge Publishing
"The Foremost in Innovative Fiction"
experimentalfiction.com

JEF Books are distributed to the book trade by
SPD: Small Press Distribution
and to the academic journal market by EBSCO

table of contents

the haircut

Later as he would think about the events of that day Kurt Lang couldn't help feeling the reason for what had happened to him was the fact he was thinking about Ionesco's *The Lesson* as he was walking into the barbershop—he had an image of a male figure lying on its side on the floor in the fetal position with its arms and knees pressed to its chest protecting the guts spilling out of its ripped-open belly. He suppressed the vision instantly however so that it barely registered in his mind and calmly walked over to the row of chairs standing against the wall on the left to await his turn. The only barber in the shop—a woman—was working on a customer in the barber's chair next to the door.

But he didn't have to wait. As soon as he sat down the curtain on the door in the back of the room stirred and another woman stepped out from behind it, walked up to the last—third—barber's chair, and motioned for him to sit in it. He stood up and started toward it.

After a few steps his feet in their hard-heeled cowboy half-boots slipped on the bare wooden floor however and he almost fell down, stopping himself at the last moment with his left arm. He realized then that the floor in the barbershop wasn't level as he had assumed but sloped up at a not insignificant angle toward the back which must have been the reason for his slipping. He turned red from embarrassment and exertion, mumbled something that was a cross between a curse and an apology, stood up, and treading carefully with his feet at an angle so that the edges of his boots dug themselves into the floor walked toward the chair at which the woman waited for him. She stood with no expression on her face as if she hadn't seen what had happened or found it insignificant, made room for him to get into the chair, and covered him with a barber cloth that she seemed to have produced literally out of thin air. It was of a hideous reddish-brown color with tiny red flowers all over it and was made from the same material as the curtain on the door from which she had come out.

The woman was tall and skinny with a bony masculine frame and a huge mop of reddish-brown hair on her head of a color not unlike that of the curtain and the cloth she had draped over Kurt. She spoke with an extremely heavy foreign accent which Kurt found impossible to understand and suspected of being Russian. He explained to himself she was a recent immigrant to the country, possibly an illegal one, either from Russia or one of the former republics of the Soviet Union. A sharp acrid odor emanated from her which reminded Kurt of formic acid and which he ascribed to her having a bad case of acid stomach. He loved leveling ant heaps in his youth and he remembered them smelling like this as he would dig them up with a stick, an inexplicable fury inside him driving him on.

The woman said something to Kurt as she was fastening the cloth around his neck. He didn't understand what it was but from the context of his situation assumed she had asked what kind of haircut he wanted. He stirred under the cloth, stuck his left hand out, touched his hair with his fingers, and said he wanted it cut short but not too much so. He had let his hair grow long over the winter and now that warm weather was coming he wanted it shorter. Without any sign of acknowledgment she understood him the woman set to work and Kurt proceeded to make himself comfortable in the chair.

It seemed to tilt to the right with the floor for he found himself sliding in that direction on the slippery upholstered plastic seat.

14

He moved himself up a few times supporting his body with his hands on the armrests and eventually found himself sitting with his fingers dug into them. The woman noticed this, said something again, stuck her hand under the cloth, and pulled out one end of a safety belt like those on an airplane. She was apparently suggesting for Kurt to strap himself in. Surprised though that he was he followed the woman's suggestion, strapped himself in tightly, and found the solution worked. He no longer slid down. Finally free to do so, he sank into that half-sleep state one usually settles in when in a barber's chair and waited for the woman to finish her job.

She worked fast. The scissors flew furiously around his head as if chasing the comb that kept eluding them hiding time and time again in his hair. Kurt saw big clumps of hair fly off his head in all directions as if fleeing it in haste like the proverbial rats a sinking ship. Eventually this brought him back to reality and he realized with surprise the strange person looking at him out of the mirror was he—the woman was giving him a much shorter haircut than he had wanted. But she was clearly not finished yet and it was going to get shorter.

A wave of panic came over Kurt. He turned hot, stirred again under the cloth, stuck out his left hand, and said to the woman she was cutting his hair too short. She ignored him however as if not having heard him or finding what he had said unworthy of consideration and went on working at the same furious pace. Kurt was going to stop her but decided not to. He was sure she had a plan she was following and stopping her would most likely lead to even worse results than letting her go on. With terror in his heart he watched his hair continue flying off his head as if panic-stricken trying to get away from it as far away and as quickly as possible and a progressively more and more strange-looking person staring him in the face out of the mirror before him.

15

Then at one moment he realized with consternation there was a big, fist-sized hollow in his right temple which he had never noticed. Or did he notice it once but had been hiding it under his hair, having purposely pushed the awareness of it out of his mind? This must have been the case. He had always worn his hair longer than most men and didn't he complain about the hollow in his temple to his parents once as a kid and they told him he would have to cover it up with his hair? He had a vague recollection of something like that happening. But he looked strange in other ways too. His cheek bones seemed higher than he remembered and his eyes glittered in an Oriental fashion under his thick black eyebrows now left to fend for themselves by the hair that had left his head. Did he have Asian blood in him?... Or perhaps Mexican?... They never talked about their origins in his family and one of his uncles was quite dark and was called Xavier....

Kurt grew hot all over again and felt sweat stand out on his skin. Soon he saw it glitter on the face of the unhappy-looking Asian or Latin American man with a deformed skull staring at him out of the mirror as if in solidarity with his shiny Oriental eyes.

The woman kept working on his hair at the same frantic pace and his head looked more and more punched in on the right like a pillow hit with a fist while his face displayed progressively more and more pronounced non-European features. But realizing there was nothing he could do about it and moreover that nothing truly significant was being done to him—the scissors in the woman's hands weren't changing him but were merely revealing his true nature—he resigned himself to his fate, that is to the image of himself that would emerge after the woman was through cutting his hair and waited for this to happen.

Finally after shaving his temples and the back of his neck with an electric razor the woman was finished. Kurt was devastated. His

16

face looked pathetically naked and vulnerable like a chicken plucked of its feathers while still alive. When the woman took the cloth off him, wiped his neck clean, and brushed the hair off his jacket, he unbuckled the safety belt, got out of the chair, and paid her with a large bill. He had debated whether or not to tip her but at the last moment to his surprise gave her a much bigger tip out of the change she brought him back than he customarily gave barbers, wanting to prove more to himself than to her that he bore her no grudge for what she had done, and walked toward the outside door. The customer in the first chair was gone but there was a huge pile of hair on the floor around the chair and the woman barber that had worked on him was getting ready to sweep it up. It looked as though there were clothes mixed in with it as if the man had been divested of them together with his hair as part of the haircut. Kurt got curious what the floor around the chair he had sat in looked like but the prospect scared him. He had a feeling there would be a puddle of blood spreading out from under the hair that lay there as if from under his own limp form.

On stepping out into the street contrary to what he had planned originally Kurt turned left in the direction opposite to where he had come from and continued along the sidewalk. It was as if he hoped to undo through this what had happened in the barbershop by pretending he hadn't gone into it but had merely strolled by. This didn't change the facts however. The nakedness around his skull was like a loud ringing in his ears which was making it hard for him to perceive the world around him. The skin along his temples stung like fingernails cut too short. This made him think at first of the stinging you feel when an ant bites you but then he noticed a similar sensation coming from the tips of his fingers. His heart sank. Did the woman cut his fingernails too? Quickly he brought up his right hand, looked at his fingers, and saw the nails on them were cut so close blood was showing from under some of them in places. As if hoping to prove this wrong he looked at his left hand

17

but saw the situation there was the same. The woman had trimmed the fingernails on both his hands without him noticing it! It must have happened when he was dozing in the chair having settled down in comfort after strapping himself in. Outraged, he stopped and was about to turn around, walk back to the barbershop, and give the woman a piece of his mind, but stopped himself and continued walking. What good would that do? Would he ask the woman to give him back his money? He was sure she wouldn't do it and besides what difference would that make? It was a piddling amount and it wouldn't undo the damage she had done. He couldn't sue her for damages because what she had done wasn't that terrible and she could always say he could have stopped her cutting his fingernails had he wanted to. She might have even asked him if he wanted her to do it and when he didn't answer she assumed he did. It was his fault. He shouldn't have dozed off. He recalled then hearing or reading somewhere it was a common practice in some countries in Europe for barbers to trim their customers' fingernails as part of giving them a haircut. So that must have been the reason why she did it. She clearly wasn't well adapted to this country and thought everything here was the same as where she came from. There was no point in his complaining. He had to forget what had happened and get on with his life.

He recalled then hearing or reading at the same time he heard or read about the custom with cutting fingernails that it was also a common practice in those countries for barbers to trim their clients' eyebrows. Did she trim his? He raised his right hand to touch his eyebrows to check if this is what had happened but realized it was unnecessary. When he saw in the mirror the final plucked-chicken-image of himself as he was getting out of the chair, in place of the two fat leaches of his eyebrows which had always been the source of pride for him and admiration of some of his friends there were two pale gray stains like shadows cast by

18

two small clouds hovering above his forehead. He had been too shocked then to react to it. Still he touched his forehead with his fingers and felt under them the short prickly hairs left there as he expected.

Surprisingly he felt better. He realized then his pants legs felt strange around his boots. They seemed shorter and his calves felt as if cold air was getting to them. Did the woman trim his pants legs too? Apparently she did. He didn't bother looking down to check this but walked on. Another little thing like that made no difference.

He came to the intersection and stopped since the light was red his way. It turned green almost instantly, he resumed walking, got to the other side of the street, and continued along the sidewalk.

The houses on the other side of the street on his right were all unnaturally tall and thin like drawings on a rubber membrane that has been stretched too much and on his left low and leaning in one direction like teeth in a comb someone broke by pushing down hard on them. The sky above his head was gone. It was then he realized that his apartment which lay behind his back and to which he was eventually bound to return was a long and narrow space looking like a bowling alley, its upper left corner dissolving in the void as in a fog.

dead darling

"Imagination dead, imagine . . ."
Samuel Beckett

A room in a hospital where bodies are kept or in a police morgue. Tall walls lined with white tiles that look gray and shine like viscera. Similar but not identical white tiles on the floor. In the back two huge stainless-steel refrigerators for storing bodies, apparently three in each, closed. To the left and right stainless-steel doors, also closed. In the center a stainless-steel cart with black plastic wheels for transporting bodies, covered with a green sheet that hangs down to the floor on the sides, empty. On the right, attached to the wall, a white ceramic sink that looks white for a change. A set of lights mounted in the ceiling cast a strong vertical white light that makes everything beneath it look worthless like a powerful analytical mind driven by a cynical personality.

A man, middle aged, of average height and build, dressed in a tan or gray suit (it is hard to tell which in the overly bright light) and a loose gray or khaki raincoat (also hard to tell which), open, paces nervously back and forth behind the cart, a cellular phone like a tiny severed hand already black pressed to his left ear. He speaks in an exasperated desperate voice as if hoping that the emotion he projects will change his situation.

Man *(beside himself)*:... yes... a woman... killed or died, we don't know which.... Was supposed to be in room number 13... *(A long pause.)* Yes... yes. That's her. *(A pause.)* But she's not here... The

23

cart's empty. *(A long pause.)* No, I haven't ... Alright, I'll look. Wait, hold on. I want to have you on the line.

He goes up to the first refrigerator, the one on the left, and opens the door. The inside is divided into three horizontal compartments, one close above the other like bunk beds in a concentration camp. They are stuffed full with articles of food such as bags of flour, pasta, and sugar, cans of vegetables, meats, and soups, bottles of soda, vinegar, oil, soy sauce, boxes of cereals and crackers, bread in plastic bags, and so on, as well as household items of various kinds, among them, salt and pepper shakers, trivets, candlesticks, an electric coffee mill, a toaster, a tea kettle, a wire dish rack, what looks like two separate sets of dishes, a large stainless steel basin, pots and pans, kitchen utensils, loose and on a rack, a birdcage, empty, an aquarium, also empty, a butterfly net, a set of wine glasses, two electric fans, one a table model, another one freestanding, lying on its side, an electric iron, an ironing board, a plastic bucket, a mop, a broom, a dustpan, and a few throw rugs, neatly rolled up. The man runs his eyes over the things, but surprisingly isn't surprised by them and speaks calmly into the phone.

Man: There's no body here, just junk. Wait, I'll look in the other one.

He shuts the door, goes over to the second refrigerator and opens its door. It is constructed exactly as the first one and is also stuffed full with household items except these are mostly toilet and bedroom articles such as a scale, a bathroom stool lying on its side, a rubber bath mat, neatly rolled up, bottles of shampoo, lotion, and toilet water, many bars of soap in a wicker basket, a plastic wastebasket, a long-handled brush for scrubbing one's back, two pillows without pillowcases, what looks like half a dozen sets of bed linen, blankets, towels, and two bathrobes, all haphazardly piled up. The man again runs his eyes over the things, again isn't surprised by them, and speaks calmly into the phone.

Man: She's not here either, just junk. That's it... There're only two refrigerators.

As he speaks he turns around and walks toward the cart. Now he can see under it through its open end and apparently notices something unusual there because he gets animated, runs up to the cart, kneels down, and lifts the edge of the sheet on his side. He speaks in an excited voice into the phone.

Man: I think she's here... under the cart... Yes!... Oh, my God! She's dead!

He puts the phone on the floor face up without turning it off and pushes the cart to the right, exposing the body of a woman lying on her right side, in other words facing him, in the fetal position. She is dressed in a yellow bikini with white polka dots.

A tiny Lilliputian voice is heard coming out of the phone shouting something and sounding ludicrous in this situation. It does this a few times and then stops abruptly as if realizing its own inadequacy. The person has apparently hung up. After a few seconds the phone starts beeping out a busy signal. Lilliputian though it also is, it is annoying like the dripping of a faucet. The man doesn't seem to hear it however.

In the meantime he has covered the woman's body with his, embracing it. He rolls it over on its back in the process. The body, surprisingly, uncurls easily and naturally. It lies with its legs stretched out and the arms along the torso, appearing to be alive. The man unexpectedly straightens up and holding the woman by the shoulders shouts at her.

Man: You're alive! But they told me you were dead!

The woman is in fact alive. She wears a pair of slanted, white-framed sunglasses which give her an exotic, oriental air. Her pubic region bulges unnaturally high under her bathing suit, as if padded with something. She tries to free herself from the man's hands, motioning with her arms for him to lean back. After the man has let go of her and straightens up she points at the ceiling indicating she wants him not to shade her from the light. It becomes apparent then that she is lying on a large white bathmat as if on a beach towel. She speaks in an aloof voice, as if physically far away.

Woman: You're keeping the light from me. I'm tanning myself.

The man is clearly astounded at what he sees and hears. He looks at the woman in disbelief, unable to say a word. The sound of a melody being hummed comes from somewhere, most probably from the woman. From the snippets that can be heard it appears to be the song "Mary Ann" popularized by Harry Belafonte in the 1950s. The Lilliputian beeping sound coming from the phone once again becomes audible. For a few seconds the man continues disregarding it but in the end hears it, turns to the phone, picks it up, turns it off, and puts it in the breast pocket of his jacket. He is finally over his amazement and speaks to the woman.

Man: Where have you been? What happened?

The woman lies still for a while and then answers reluctantly.

Woman: You always want to know everything ... too much... I'm here now. Isn't it enough?

Man (exasperated): But they called me and said you were dead!

26

Woman *(with profound irony, scoffing)*: What do they know? They were wrong, as you can plainly see. I'm very much alive. *(After a pause she adds, clarifying her last statement.)* I answer to nobody. I do as I please.

She stirs finally as if to make herself comfortable, moving her head from side to side, repositioning her arms, pulling up her left leg and keeping it bent at the knee, and giving a big sigh, indicating her impatience or displeasure with the situation. Then suddenly she sits up almost hitting the man on the chin with her head in the process. He leans back just in time.

Woman *(annoyed in the extreme)*: What's the point?... It's regular light, not ultraviolet. I can't get a tan here.

She looks around the room breathing angrily, her nostrils flaring, as if looking for something, but apparently doesn't find it, stands up, goes up to the first refrigerator, opens it, takes out the stainless steel basin, not looking for it but locating it immediately, obviously knowing where it is, shuts the door, goes over to the second refrigerator, opens it, takes a hand towel out of one of the stacks of towels, which is white, shuts the door, goes over to the sink, hangs the towel over her left shoulder, fills the basin with water, waiting for it to get warm, and puts the basin on the floor. The man in the meantime has stood up, followed the woman with his eyes as she moved around, and is now looking at her with interest.

Facing the wall the woman squats over the basin, hangs the towel over the edge of the sink, and with her left hand pulls aside the crotch of the bikini so as to expose her sex. As she does this a large wad of money falls out of the bikini into the basin. It was this that made her pubic region bulge so high. The woman catches it immediately with her right hand, curses quietly, shakes the water

27

off of it onto the floor, stuffs it in her bra, and starts washing herself off, using her right hand. The water makes a soft, melodious sound, splashing against the metal basin, like that of a harpsichord. The man continues watching the woman silently, again as if in disbelief. Crouching over the basin the woman looks like a female dog urinating, squatting close to the ground. She takes a long time washing off, obviously wanting to make sure she has done a good job, but eventually she is done, stands up, still holding the crotch of the bikini to the side, her knees bent a little, reaches out with her right hand for the towel, takes it, and dries herself off. Having done it she hangs the towel over the edge of the sink, takes the money out of her bra, holds it firmly in her right hand, walks to the door on the right, opens it, and walks out, leaving the door open.

There is total darkness behind the door which falls into the room like a huge shaft of antilight. The woman disappears. A blast of cold air is blown inside and with it a few snowflakes that dance wistfully in the air as if looking for a companion and being unable to find one. Eerie electronic music is heard at the same time coming in through the door that seems black as the darkness and cold as the cold air, an apt accompaniment to the woman's disappearance and the dancing of snowflakes. The man stands looking at the empty door in amazement. His coat blows in the air that streams into the room. After a while his whole body starts swaying in the stream of air as if he were just his clothes, empty on the inside. Then he too starts dancing, whirling through the room. At one point he collides with the cart and tries to use it as his dancing partner but has little luck with it. Then he is blown over to the second refrigerator and thrown against the door. Rebounding from it he opens it and takes out of it the plastic wastebasket, which is white, shuts the door, dances over to the cart, places the wastebasket in the middle of it, dances over to the first refrigerator, opens its door, finds in the clutter inside it a long, dried-out lily stalk, shuts the door, dances over to the cart, and puts the lily stalk in it as in a vase. Then he dances over to the second refrigerator and takes a few items out of it such as brushes with long handles or other long things, shuts the door, dances over to the cart, and puts the things in the wastebasket as he had done with the lily. After that he dances over to the first refrigerator again, opens it, takes a bunch of things out of it to complement what he has put in the wastebasket, shuts the door, dances over to the cart, and arranges the things there. He repeats this process a few times, alternating between the two refrigerators until he is satisfied with the arrangement he has created. It constitutes a pitiful ikebana of the memory of the woman who has gone away. While taking the things from the refrigerators to the cart the man sometimes presses them to his heart as if to indicate how dear they are to him or how much he values the purpose they will serve. While dancing over to the refrigerators he sometimes covers his face with his hands, hanging his head down or throwing it back, expressing through these gestures the sadness he feels at the woman's disappearance. His face grows more and more pale and blank with time and eventually streams with tears. It looks like a windowpane flowing with rain.

The wind has suddenly grown stronger. It whistles, drowning out the music. The door closes with a tremendous bang. The man continues dancing however as if not having noticed what has happened. Apparently he wasn't dancing to the music but to a tune in his mind that must have been very similar to the music. He covers his face with his hands, hangs his head down, throws it back, and cries as before.

As soon as the door closes, something red starts seeping into the room from under the doors on both sides, covering the floor. It is blood. The man dances in it, apparently not noticing what is happening. His feet make unpleasant smacking sounds on the bloody tiles like lips trying to say something but being unable to do it. The blood keeps rising. It reaches the man's ankles, then knees. He has a hard time dancing, but continues trying. He covers his face with his hands and cries less and less however devoting more and more of his energy and attention to the task of moving. The woman must have splashed a lot of water out of the basin because it floats easily in the blood. A black coffin and its lid now appear, floating in separately. Unlikely as it seems they must have somehow floated into the room from under one of the doors. They bob up and down and sway from side to side as if making overtures to the basin which blithely ignores them. The man also ignores the things. It's as if they don't exist. The blood has risen up to his waist. He can no longer pretend he is dancing but continues to move, turning around slowly. Now he has stopped showing his grief altogether and devotes all of his energy and attention to moving. The skirt of his coat has gathered like excrement around him. The excrement seems to be his. The blood keeps rising. The towel floats aimlessly through the room, not knowing what to do. The wastebasket that serves as a vase tries to float too but tips over and its contents spill out. Some of these float in the blood, others sink to the bottom. Eventually the wastebasket does the same. The sheet that covered the cart has finally risen and floats in the blood as if looking for a place to sink.

The room now starts expanding. The walls grow wider and taller as if fleeing, unable to stand each other. The ceiling also rises and disappears. The refrigerators detach themselves from the wall, grow tall, expand, and float in the blood. Blood has risen almost up to the man's chin. He has stopped moving and seems to be choked by his coat. Finally he apparently starts moving his legs, for he rises. Standing up he takes off his coat, then his jacket, finally his tie, and starts swimming. The last glimpse of his face shows it to be completely empty—not like a blank sheet of paper but a sheet of paper virtually all of which has been cut out except

30

for a thin rim around its perimeter. The room is now a sea of blood with the walls a white sky on the horizon on all sides. The refrigerators sway from side to side and bob up and down tall like office towers made of stainless steel. The man swims with an expert crawl stroke keeping his head above the blood, staring toward a spot on the horizon where his heart, huge as the sun, throbs laboriously, trying to rise into the sky.

agamemnon post mortem

It must be a stage because it is elevated, lit up, and hung with black cloth on the sides, the back, and overhead. It is huge though, some two hundred feet wide, one hundred deep, and fifty tall. All of the above seems fitting for the event that took place and continues taking place there now.

Four sounds are heard coming from the right side of the stage behind the curtain, most likely echoes of events of the past superimposed upon each other, gradually dying away. They overlap occasionally, nearly drowning out themselves, while sounding loud and clear the rest of the time during gaps of silence in their companions. The first sound resembles the moan of a person engaged in something strenuous but brief which goes over into a sigh of relief that appears to be both physical and psychological. The second sound is a sibilant swishing noise that turns into a crunching one like something sharp moving fast through the air, entering soft matter, passing through it, striking something hard, and shattering it. The third sound is similar to the bellowing of a bull being butchered magnified many times. It could also be a human voice, male, very deep, imitating the bellowing of a bull being butchered. The fourth sound is that of water splashing as if something big had fallen into it and then hitting a thin metal wall and making it ring with the sound of a harpsichord. These appear to be respectively the echoes of the sounds made by a person wielding an ax in the process of striking something with it; an ax flying through the air, hitting soft tissue, entering it, striking a bone, and shattering it; a person hit by an ax crying out in pain; and a person's body slumping into water and the water splashing against the sides of the vessel it is in. The situation fits

35

the event of Agamemnon being killed by his wife Clytemnestra together with her lover, Agamemnon's cousin Aegisthus, while taking a bath.

The sounds decay unnaturally slowly as if recorded and then played back at slow speed, it being clear that it will take them a long time to die away completely. This goes on for a while and then new sounds are heard coming from the same direction superimposed on the original ones. These are high-pitched squeaky noises resembling those made by mice rummaging around or people's voices recorded and played back at fast speed. After a while it becomes certain these are people's voices—two persons arguing about something. The argument goes on and at one point becomes heated so that it seems the people will come to blows. But then unexpectedly it stops and is followed by normal conversation—the people have reached an agreement. Soon the conversation stops altogether and is followed by sounds appearing to be preparations for something complex to take place—people walk back and forth, talk to each other, move heavy objects, bang on things, and so on. Then unexpectedly again a high-pitched voice shrieks something that appears to be a command. It resembles a military command in highly authoritarian countries such as Prussia or imperial Russia. A great sighing is heard then seemingly by a number of people in unison, then a loud sigh of relief, and a very loud noise consisting of a brief squishing period followed by a longer crunching one. These four sounds—the command, the sighing, the relief, and the squishing with the crunching—are repeated once and then again and again. It seems something huge is being hacked up by a group of people wielding an ax together under the command of someone with a squeaky voice. The hacking continues directed by commands but then these stop and the hacking goes on by itself. It looks as though those performing the hacking have mastered it enough so that they can do it by themselves. When the hacking stops it is followed by a series of new directions by the squeaky voice which in turn are followed by the sounds of people walking around, moving heavy objects, and so on, similar to those heard earlier. Some other activity is taking place behind the curtains also strenuous at times but of a different nature. When it stops, the squeaky voice is heard again giving a command, then counting off that must be "one-two, one-two" in some strange language on the background of the sound of footsteps of many people walking in step, and onto the stage comes out from behind the curtains on the right a tiny midget-sized figure dressed in a full-length pink gown followed by a group of some twenty normal-sized men dressed in rags carrying a huge object on a wooden litter supported on their shoulders. At the end of the procession walks another similar midget figure dressed in a black gown. The first figure must be a man because his hair is short and the second one a woman for her hair is long. The man's hair is curly and golden and it molds itself gracefully to his skull; the woman's long, wavy, and black. The object the men carry is weird in a frightening way—black, white, and red, of an ill-defined shape which cannot be recognized as anything common. The procession marches sternly forward to the left side of the stage and then it becomes apparent what the object is—it is the upper quarter of an enormous human head, apparently that of a man because the hair is short, the eyebrow thick, and the nose and ear fleshy.

The midget man walks all the way to the left back corner of the stage, stops there, steps aside, and marching in place points where the men are to put down the part of the head. They stop, lower the litter, and tilt it toward the back of the stage so that the part of the head slides off onto the floor. It rests on the ear and sways for a while like a quarter of a watermelon lying on its curved side. The midget man counts off for a time while marching in place but seeing that the men don't and can't follow his counting stops doing it and watches what they do with interest. The woman joins him and the two stand together their shoulders touching. The woman puts her arm around the man's shoulder; he—his around her waist. They are clearly pleased with what they see. When the men have finished with the head the midget man disengages himself from the woman and shouts a series of commands at them. They pick up the litter and carry it off the stage to where they have come from. The man leads the way again marching in step with them, raising his feet unnaturally high and counting off. The woman follows the procession as she did when it came out onto the stage.

New sounds of hacking, straining, and lifting are heard once again behind the curtains followed by a command and counting off and soon another procession comes out onto the stage exactly as before. This time they carry the second upper quarter of the head and deposit it next to the first one in the same fashion. Everything else is done again exactly as before except that the couple don't put their arms around each other—the joy stemming from their accomplishment has apparently worn off.

It is clear that we are witnessing the events after the killing of Agamemnon by Clytemnestra and Aegisthus—she is the midget woman and he the midget man. Agamemnon's body is being chopped up behind the curtains and then stacked on the stage. The two remaining quarters of the head are brought out first. Then come the arms. After that the first and second part of one of the legs. And then in the following order upper left chest, part of the second leg, more of the chest, the rest of the second leg, and the first and second part of the rest of the torso, all huge and hairy.

During the third appearance on the stage Aegisthus marches in front of the procession, counting off and Clytemnestra follows it as before. During the fourth appearance they lead the procession together without Aegisthus's counting off. Everyone walks out of step. After the men deposit the quarter of the head Aegisthus orders them backstage and Clytemnestra and he remain on it and look at the parts of the head that are there. The last quarter has been put on top of one of the others. The couple talk to each other apparently debating whether the situation with the fourth quarter of the head sitting on top of another one is stable. It does look in fact precarious. They apparently feel it is stable enough though, stop talking, and wait for the men to do their job.

The men now come out onto the stage alone bringing out body parts in the indicated order. Aegisthus and Clytemnestra remain on the stage until the first part of the chest is brought out. Then they go back together. Clytemnestra comes back very soon thereafter before the men return with another body part and looks for something on the floor where she and Aegisthus had stood which she apparently feels she must have dropped. She doesn't find it and walks off the stage. Aegisthus comes out a little later after the men have come out and tells them where to put the particular body part (part of the first leg). He walks off the stage with the men. While doing this at one point he stops abruptly, bends down, and picks up something thin and shiny from the floor. It must be the object Clytemnestra looked for—a pin or an earring most probably. From then on the men keep bringing out the body parts and put them down on the stage by themselves.

With the body being chopped up and its being so big it stands to reason that there must be much blood. It does in fact eventually find its way onto the stage—when the men start bringing out parts of the torso a smacking sound is heard, as if with lips trying to say something but unable to do it, which is caused by their feet treading in the blood. The men eventually notice this and they step in a gingerly fashion, sometimes on their toes and sometimes heels. When the second part of Agamemnon's chest has been brought out onto the stage Aegisthus appears again to check on

39

the progress. He is clearly aware of the blood because he is on stilts and moves stiffly holding onto them with his hands. He must have had a fair amount of practice with the stilts because he moves with ease and confidence. When all of the body has been brought out both Aegisthus and Clytemnestra come out onto the stage, each of them on stilts. They look over the stage, making sure that everything has been done properly, are pleased with what they see, and go off the stage not to appear again. The men also don't come out onto the stage so that it remains empty except for Agamemnon's chopped up body.

The body parts have been placed more or less randomly all over the stage. Most of them have been placed directly onto the floor, most probably because it was difficult to stack them on top of each other and because they would have not been stable in such positions. The exceptions are the fourth quarter of the head mentioned earlier and some of the parts of the limbs which have been put in heaps. As a consequence of this the stage looks cluttered. It is like a room in an apartment or house into which new tenants are moving in after the movers have brought in the crates but before these have been attended to. It seems this still has to take place. Because of this an air of uncertainty reigns over the stage as during the proverbial waiting for the second shoe to drop after the dropping of the first one. One wonders what will take place there next.

Silence reigns behind the curtains after Aegisthus and Clytemnestra walk off the stage. The only sound heard is the dying away of the echoes mentioned at the beginning. They are still audible but it is clear that soon they will die away completely. It seems that everyone backstage has gone away. This isn't so however—suddenly a bed is heard creaking. The couple are apparently turning in for the night. They fidget around for a while as people normally do before going to sleep and then silence falls.

It looks as though the two have gone to sleep. But this isn't so again. The bed starts creaking once more, this time in a rhythmic fashion—"creak-creak, creak-creak"—leaving little doubt as to what is going on backstage. The creaking is even for a while, then speeds up, slows down, stops altogether, resumes, and so on— the usual sequence in such situations. Eventually it ends as always with a stretch of rapid sounds which stop abruptly, are followed by silence, then irregular creaking sounds, and finally silence for good. The couple have satisfied their natural needs and have gone to sleep.

When the rhythmic creaking has gone on for a while, a new sound emerges becoming audible even on the background of the sounds of the echoes. It is a male voice, full and clear as the ringing of a perfectly cast bell. It sings a song, a rousing, rhythmic one, apparently a military march. The voice grows stronger with time but is drowned out for a while by the rapid creaking that comes at the end mentioned earlier. When silence descends backstage the voice has grown quite strong, drowning out almost completely the sounds of the echoes. It is the voice of Agamemnon released from his chopped-up body—brain—where it had been stored. It must have come out of it like vapor, has drifted around aimlessly for a while, searched for its parts to join together, and has now coalesced into a whole. The song naturally is in ancient Greek and sings of powerful sandaled feet marching along dusty roads, hard rocks, and soft grassy fields, of the flashing of copper spears like that of lightning bolts, of the blinding gleam of bronze swords like rays of the sun, of the flare of conflagrations reflected in the convex surfaces of shields, breastplates, and helmets, of white limestone walls of enemy towns crumbling, knocked down like teeth knocked out by the sharp handle of a sword, of the enemy's women wailing but secretly craving the powerful bodies of the victors, of a warm splash of the enemy's blood licking dog-fashion the victor's foot.

41

The song ends. Silence follows on the background of the almost completely decayed sounds of the echoes. One thinks then that Agamemnon's voice will not be heard again. But this isn't so. Soon it comes back stronger and clearer than before, speaking. It addresses someone, a crowd most likely, probably his soldiers in the camp on the Aegean shore plagued by pestilence while awaiting the departure for Troy, exhorts them to be steadfast, manly, not to forget their duty, then a more intimate gathering, probably the leaders in his tent, by the light of torches, his voice harsh yet warm, the logic in his speech clear as a simple figure drawn on a slate. Then come stern words, clearly addressed to one person, his daughter Iphigenia obviously, advising her of her fate, reminding her of her and his duty. After that is heard a hoarse sobbing and words muffled by a twisted, knotted tongue as by a blanket bitten into—his crying in the solitude of the dark tent before the morning when he would have to do his terrible duty. Then come peaceful words that speak of a beautiful city with straight wide streets, spacious squares with tall statues, gracefully proportioned buildings inhabited by an enlightened, civilized people—his imagined state—of surrounding landscapes with rolling hills and gentle valleys seductive like a woman's body under a thin shirt, of orchards white and pink like girls in bloom in the springtime, of verdant meadows with brooks like silver jewelry lying in the grass, of blinding gold wheat fields against a frighteningly blue sky, of the sea like a monstrously huge horse impatiently pawing the sand, tossing its white knotted mane, and finally of man, the male, always alone, his body his sole companion, constantly marching forward down the empty road of life toward the goal of his duty on the far side of the horizon, hoping to put more distance between himself and the stern figure of tragedy draped in a black toga—the tragic sense of life—inside him, a feeling no woman will ever understand.

The sound of the words has grown faint. The energy that was behind them has almost run out. They have merged with the echoes and continue decaying with them. Within minutes total silence will reign on the stage. Then however new sounds are heard coming from behind the curtains on the right—the same high-pitched squeaky noises as earlier, clearly the midgets' voices. At first there is heard a higher-pitched voice, obviously Clytemnestra's, asking something, then after a while a lower-pitched one—Aegisthus's—answers reluctantly, then Clytemnestra speaks again in a censuring tone, a muffled grumbling from Aegisthus follows, and is followed in turn by creaking noises, apparently those of the bed. Clytemnestra appears to have asked Aegisthus if he had done something, he answered that he hadn't, she scolds him for that and urges him to do it now, he reluctantly obeys her, and gets out of bed. The conjecture turns out to be true—Aegisthus appears from behind the curtains on the right sleepy-eyed and with tousled hair wearing a plain long white shirt—a nightgown—and proceeds walking across the stage. He apparently has to do something there. He has forgotten about blood being on the stage and is not walking on stilts. Having made a few steps he realizes this, stops, lifts up one of his feet, looks at it, sees it is all bloody, but decides it is too late to do anything about it and continues on his way. After a few steps he gets up on his toes however obviously bothered too much by the blood. This apparently isn't much of an improvement for soon he switches to walking on his heels. He appears to like it better for he continues walking this way. He walks slowly seemingly not quite awake, putting his heels down hard on the floor and making thumping noises with them. At one point he apparently grows aware of an unpleasant smell for he holds his nose with his fingers and continues walking this way from then on. The smell must come from the chopped-up body which may have started to decompose already. Aegisthus lets go of his nose a few times but the smell is clearly too strong and in the end he continues holding it as he

43

moves across the stage. Also after walking on his heels for good part of the way he grows tired of it and switches back to his toes but still likes it less and soon switches again to his heels. It is walking in this fashion and holding his nose that he reaches the other side of the stage. When he gets there he stops. It becomes clear then that there is a parting in the curtain in that spot and that behind the curtain there is a wall. On it there is a light switch. The midgets have forgotten to turn off the lights on the stage. It is hard for Aegisthus to stand on his heels while reaching up and besides the switch is a little high for him to reach so he switches back to his toes. Then he lifts his free hand and flips the switch. The lights on the stage go out. Total darkness descends on it. All the sounds have decayed now and silence reigns everywhere. Then one can hear Aegisthus's footsteps—he has turned around and is walking back across the stage. From the sound his feet make it is clear he is walking flat-footed. He seems to have ceased to care about the blood. It is as if his not seeing it made it easier for him to do it. Aegisthus makes a steady if slow progress across the stage. Even though he moves in total darkness he doesn't lose his way and doesn't bump into any of the parts of the body scattered over the stage however. He reaches the curtains and goes behind them. You can hear him walk backstage, stop, clearly by the side of the bed, climb into it, and start making himself comfortable. He didn't bother wiping his feet and is anxious to continue his interrupted sleep. (What will Clytemnestra's reaction to this be in the morning is not hard to guess.) Clytemnestra's voice is then heard asking something. She obviously hasn't been asleep and wants to make sure Aegisthus has done his job. He answers grumpily, clearly saying that he has, completes making himself comfortable, and grows quiet. There is no sound from Clytemnestra. She has apparently also decided to go to sleep. The couple have satisfied all their conscious needs and are entering the realm of dreams. Silence and darkness reign everywhere.

the revenge

a potential stage piece

A long narrow hallway with an unusually high ceiling, perhaps fifteen feet tall, brightly illuminated from above with cold bluish neon light and lined on both sides with ceiling-high bookcases packed with books of frequently wildly differing sizes standing next to each other and largely in disarray (leaning this way and that, sticking out here and there, and so forth). The milky-blue light gathered in places in shallow puddles on the uneven gray linoleum-covered floor like cleaning liquid after a recent washing. A tiny door fit sooner for an animal (dog) than a person, with no apparent way to open it in the wall at the end. Up front on the right a narrow two-winged door that opens out reaching almost to the ceiling. Two figures, female Ell and male Orr, she on the left, he on the right, both barefoot and dressed in identical blue-gray shirts and pants huddled against it, their ears close to it, listening to what is going on behind it. Both with short light brown hair, sunken cheeks, dark circles under their eyes, and wan complexions, of average height and slight built, extremely similar looking, almost like identical twins, except for Ell's slighter upper body, wider hips, and longer hair. The cuffs on Ell's shirt buttoned and the one on Orr's left sleeve open, apparently missing the button.

Orr *(after a long pause, in a whisper):* The squeaking has stopped.

Ell *(after a brief one, also whispering):* Like water splashing in the bathtub in which they killed our father and that girl.

Orr: And left their bodies float in it. *(After a brief pause.)* They did that, right?

47

Ell: Yes. To copulate on the floor next to the tub. She screaming in ecstasy and he gasping with exertion at the end. *(After a brief pause, hissing.)* A bitch in heat and an ever-ready cur.

Orr: Our mother and her lover... our uncle... father's cousin. *(After a brief pause.)* She barely made a squeak this time, and he just sighed... relieved, the ordeal was over.

Ell *(raising her voice):* It's boredom.... Seven years of sharing the same bed. Pleasure grows sleazy with time like cloth with wear.

Orr *(pressing the index finger of his right hand to his lips):* Shhh.... They'll hear us.

Ell *(back to a whisper, her rage not fitting in it like a square peg in a round hole):* We must let them go to sleep... their bodies float... grow weak in the warm water of their dreams.

Orr *(picking up Ell's train of thought):* Never to wake up again.

Ell: They will wake up... barely... for a few brief moments... to understand what's happening... who's come to exact the price for their monstrous crime.... Daughter and son of their murdered father.

Orr *(raising his voice):* Yes. They'll know me even though they've never seen me a grown man.

Ell *(pressing the finger of her right hand to her lips):* Shhh. Quiet. *(After a brief pause.)* Yes, they will. Their guilt will tell them who you are. *(After a longer pause, straightening up and looking over her shoulder to the back of the hallway.)* Where's Pyll? He should be here by now.

Or *(raising his head and looking in the same direction as Ell):* He will be soon…. Hasn't found the things…. They're not easy to find.

Ell in the meantime has bent down again and has brought her ear close to the door. Concentrates on the sounds coming from behind it.

Ell *(interrupting Orr):* Shhh. I think they've gone to sleep…. He's snoring. Can you hear it?

Orr *(returning back to his previous position; after a brief pause):* Yes. You're right. Or at least I think it's him. *(After a brief pause.)* Does   mother… I mean she… does she snore?

Ell: Sometimes… delicately… like a cat purring…. But mostly she moans… tortured by guilt in her dreams… figures that come to visit her… the bloody body of our father and of that poor mad girl. *(After a pause.)* But it's him snoring now for sure… asleep. *(After a pause.)* And now she's gone to sleep too. She's breathing heavily. *(After a pause.)* Can you hear it?

Orr *(after a brief pause):* Yes, she's asleep. *(Goes on listening for a while, then straightens up, satisfied, and looks toward the end of the hallway. Is visually relieved.)* Here's Pyll now.

A male figure has now appeared from somewhere at the end of the hallway on the left even though there is still no sign of an entrance of any kind visible there. This obviously is untrue however and there must be some kind of a door in the bookcase in that area which is merely masked by the books. It is Pyll. He is dressed exactly like Ell and Orr and looks very much like them, especially like the latter, but more like a sibling of nearly the same age or a fraternal twin than an identical one. He walks toward Ell and Orr carrying in his arms a huge white bed sheet gathered in a giant ball while clutching in his left hand a World War I style French Adrian helmet, lead-gray in color, and in the right one a rifle of the same period, reddish brown in places, as if with traces of old blood on it, with a shoulder strap and a four-sided bayonet at the end looking like a giant icepick. He has a hard time doing this and treads carefully so as not to stumble or drop one of the objects in his hands onto the floor.

Ell and Orr straighten up, the former turning around so as to face Pyll, step a few paces away from the door, and wait for him to reach them. Ell presses the index finger of her right hand to her lips to indicate for Pyll not to make noise.

Ell *(whispering even softer than before):* Shhh! They're asleep and we mustn't wake them up. *(After a pause.)* You found these?

Pyll *(in a voice matching hers):* The sheet I found in the laundry room in the basement and the rifle up in the attic. Had to look all over before I found it. It was in a corner under the roof. I'm covered head to toe with cobwebs.

It becomes clear then his clothes and face are covered with cobwebs, with something white in addition smudged over them which may be plaster or lime. Thin splinters of wood and a few bits of paper also cling to his clothes in places.

They speak in a whisper as before.

Pyll *(turning to Ell and offering with a gesture the sheet for her to take it):* Here, hold on to his. You'll need it to throw over them to make it easier for you to do your job. *(After Ell takes the bundle, turning to Orr.)* And these are for you. They'll serve you well.

Orr *(taking the helmet and rifle and looking at them; after a brief pause, also in a whisper, turning the helmet over in his hand):* A helmet? What for?

Pyll: In case they fight back, to protect you.

Orr: I don't need it. They won't fight back. They won't have time.

Ell: Take it, take it. It'll make you feel safer... fiercer at least... a warrior, avenger.

Orr *(agreeing reluctantly):* Alright. *(Puts the helmet on his head. It makes him look like a figure from ancient times with its crest, the visor, and the florid insignia up front. Lifts up the rifle and inspects it.)* But I don't need the rifle. It'll be in the way. The bayonet will do. It's good... long... almost a sword. *(Tries to take it off the rifle.)* Let me take it off. *(Manages to do it. Gives the rifle back to Pyll, while holding on to the bayonet. Brandishes it a few times aimlessly, then lifts it up in both his hands and brings them down in a fierce rapid movement.)* It's good. *(Repeats the previous motion a few more times. Is visibly satisfied.)* It's perfect. Nothing will stop it.

Ell *(preventing Orr to go on, bending down and moving closer to the door):* Shhh. Enough. Do you hear it? He's really snoring now.... He's sound asleep.

Orr *(behaving like Ell, bringing his ear close to the door):* And she too? Is she moaning yet? *(After a pause.)* No, just breathing heavily as before. But I'm sure she's asleep.

Ell *(bringing her ear close to the door too):* Yes, she is. You don't breathe like that if you're awake. *(After a brief pause.)* She doesn't moan all the time. Just occasionally. When ghosts of the past visit

51

her dreams. *(After a pause.)* They haven't come today. Aren't coming. There's no need for it. They know today their death will be avenged.

Orr *(picking up Ell's train of thought):* They're watching us from above.... Waiting to see how we collect their debt.

All three remain silent, Ell and Orr hunched up by the door in uncomfortable positions as if having turned to stone with Pyll aside, watching them.

Pyll *(finally stirring and moving closer to the door but not trying to listen in):* Should we do it now?

Ell *(firmly):* Yes. The time has come for them to pay the price.

Orr *(adjusting his helmet and lifting up the bayonet in his hand)*: I'm ready. Let's go.

Ell *(straightening up and unwrapping the sheet, offering one end of it to Orr):* Take this and let's spread it as we run. We'll throw it over them, so that they can't fight back.

Orr *(reluctant, hesitating):* But then they won't see us... won't know who has come to punish them.

Ell: No matter. They'll guess. They'll know for sure after we're through with them. Will remember it for eternity. Let's go.

Orr: Yes. Let's go. Let's push on the door together.

Ell moves to the center to make room for Pyll on her left, she and Orr make sure the sheet is spread wide, and all three step back a few paces.

Ell *(counting with the movement of her body as well as with words):* One, two, three.

They throw themselves against the door and it opens out with a loud crash. There is darkness behind it and Ell and Orr disappear in it pulling the sheet with them. Pyll remains standing in the doorway turned partly to the right, holding the rifle and looking ahead. He speaks loudly in a halting manner, turning his head farther right from time to time. After the initial loud stomping of feet wild screams of anger, fear, and pain are heard coming from the room at first those of two people, then of more, then of two again, and finally of one, eventually followed by sounds of movement of various kind—heavy breathing, footsteps, objects being moved, and so forth.

Pyll: Ell and Orr run forward. The room is dark. A huge bed bars their way. Two human shapes visible in it under white bedclothes. Merged with them. A man and a woman. Aegg and Clytt. He first then she. She sits up first. Straight up. Her eyes are round. She doesn't understand what's happening. Fear and surprise mixed in them. He raises himself lazily, his eyes squinting. She screams. A confused sound of "No" or "Orr!" She knows what's happening. He's still half-asleep. Ell and Orr reach the bed. They try to throw the sheet over it. Manage to get it only over Aegg. Orr tries to pull it farther. Ell throws herself onto the bed. Clytt scream, "Ell, Ell!" Is knocked down by Ell's body. Her screams are muffled by it. Aegg stirs under Ell. Tries to get out from under her. Orr has jumped onto the bed. Has pulled the sheet over all of it. Stands up on his knees. Raises the bayonet in his hands high up. Brings it down with all his might. Plunges it into the shape under him. Clytt's belly. She screams. A dark stain appears on the sheet. Blood. Orr raises his hands up again. Brings them down and plunges the bayonet higher up, into Clytt's chest, close to Ell's body. Another scream. Another dark stain appears on the sheet. Aegg has almost risen up under Ell. She slides off the bed. Stands up. Throws herself onto Aegg's lower body. Orr stand up higher on his knees. Leans to the left. Raises his hands very high. Plunges the bayonet into Aegg's chest. He falls back on the bed. Gives out a wild scream. Screams are coming from under and above the sheet. A churning sea of bedclothes, bodies, and screams. Orr has stood up on his feet. He's trying not to lose his balance under the heaving waves of the two bodies. He brings the bayonet down now with his right hand only. On the left and on the right. The sheet is covered with red stains. They grow like shadows in the evening but moving in all directions. The bed is a sea of white and blood-red waves. They're growing quiet. Only Ell and Orr scream now. Her screams grow softer and sparser. Die out. Only Orr screams now. His screams grow louder and more frequent. They are one long roar of pain and despair. The bodies under the sheet are quiet now. Ell sits up on her knees. Grasps Orr's knees in her arms. Tries to pull him off the bed. Screams, "Orr, stop, stop! Enough!" He resists her. Says nothing. Kicks her in the chest, head with his left foot. Goes on stabbing the bodies below him. Ell grabs his legs again. Screams, "Orr, Orr, stop, stop, stop!" Pulls him off the bed. They both fall down. Roll on the floor. The helmet flies off his head. Rolls on the floor. He drops the bayonet. Screams. One long scream. A scream of pain and despair. A scream of madness.

Pyll stops speaking, turns around, and walks away from the door. Orr's screaming continues for a while unchanged and then dies down like the sound of a siren that has been turned off. It stops completely, is followed by a brief period of silence, and then a faint whining sound like that of steam whistling while escaping through a pinhole in a pipe is heard coming from the same direction that changes volume, at times stopping completely but soon reappearing and continuing in this fashion from then on.

Pyll turns around and watches through the door what is happening on its other side. After a few moments Ell comes out walking through it, her face, hands, and clothes stained with blood, carrying in one hand the helmet that Orr had been wearing, bespattered with blood, and in the other the bayonet he had been given, red with blood from the tip to the handle. She walks slowly shuffling her feet on the floor and staring straight ahead, her eyes unfocused. She comes to where Pyll stands, stops, turns around, and looks through the door the same as he.

They stand still for a while as if waiting patiently for something and then the figure of Orr appears in the doorway carrying in his arms the sheet Pyll had brought, now soaked with blood and rolled into a ball which has grown to two or three times its original size. He staggers as he moves along as if carrying a huge stone boulder which he might drop any instant, not able to see where he is going but moving blindly ahead. For a while he makes soft whining sounds as described above but soon stops that and speaks in a monotonous, plaintive voice.

Orr: Aaaaa. Avenger of his father's death, killer of his mother. Aaaaa. Where will I find a place where I am not myself? Aaaaa. Avenger of his father's death, killer of his mother. Aaaaa. Where will I find a place where I am not myself? Aaaaa. Avenger of his father's death, killer of his mother. Aaaaa. Where will I find a place where I am not myself? Aaaaa.

He passes Pyll and Ell and continues walking and talking as above.

They turn around and follow a few steps behind him. After a few paces Ell steps up to Orr, places the helmet she is holding on his head and thrusts the bayonet in his right hand. He holds onto it even while having a hard time pressing the bloody sheet to his chest. Seeing what Ell has done, Pyll steps up to Orr and tries to

55

hang the rifle on his left shoulder. He is unable to do it however, so he gives it up and manages to wedge the rifle onto Orr's arms between his chest and the sheet. Orr tires to accommodate him in this as much as he can while walking on. Ell and Pyll walk now alongside Orr, she on the right and he on the left. Orr continues moving forward as if thinking there is room for him to go on forever.

the bucket
a potential screenplay

A large empty room with a high ceiling, light walls, and few or no windows, brightly lit up by an invisible source. The door likewise invisible throughout the length of the film. If there are windows, they could be dark or light, indicating respectively night or day, and if they change, passage of time.

Long shot from one of the corners of the room. A big wooden wardrobe with a two-winged door in the center facing the camera, standing at a slight angle, with its right side (left from the camera's viewpoint) closer to the camera. The door shut.

A man appears from the left of the camera and walks energetically toward the wardrobe, growing unnaturally smaller with each stride so that he looks puny upon reaching the wardrobe.

He is young—in his late twenties or early thirties—thin, of average or slightly above average height, with a bony face and dark unruly hair. He wears gray pants and a white shirt open at the neck and buttoned one button out of place, right sleeve loose, so that its end flaps around as he moves, but is barefoot.

Upon reaching the wardrobe, the man presses his left shoulder against the right side of the wardrobe and starts pushing on it. Visually, the bulk of the film consist of his pushing the wardrobe more or less aimlessly, usually in the center of the room and at times close to the wall but never against it, so that it is clear he is not trying to find a place for it but rather to merely move it along. The movement should be of some interest to the viewer, however. The wardrobe at times may be turned with its back to the camera, for instance, its progress through the room doesn't have to be continuous, that is, it may appear suddenly in different places, and so forth.

The film shows the man in long shots from the corner from which he has come out or in close-up shots, some very close, so that they show graphically how difficult it is for the man to carry out his task. These include his shoulder (sometimes left, at others times right) or chest pressed against the wardrobe, his hands trying to clutch it and being unable to do it, his feet slipping on the floor, his face turning red from the strain, his eye bulging like that of a horse straining while trying to pull a wagon too heavy for it and being whipped in the process, sweat standing out on his face, his wiping it off, his pushing aside the hair that has fallen over his forehead, saliva dripping out of his mouth, and so on and so forth.

The man is also shown resting at times between the bouts of pushing, breathing heavily, wiping off his face, or standing with his back pressed against the side of the wardrobe, with his feet out. A few times he opens the door and peeks inside it but closes it up quickly. The camera doesn't show what's inside.

The action in the film is accompanied by a sound track. The basic element in it is a ticking sound, exactly a second apart, at times very loud and unpleasant, like a nail striking a glass surface, at other almost inaudible and soft, like fingers hitting a pillow, their presence always there however.

The other element of the soundtrack is the reading of the text of the poem "On kicking the bucket" by a male voice, dispassionately and in an awkward manner, which tries to render the visual awkwardness of the unnaturally fragmented text. It is repeated four times.   The first reading consists of the first ¼ of the text, the second one of the first ½, the third one of the first ¾, and the fourth one the full text. That is, the text is read each time from the beginning, the second, third, and fourth reading consisting of appending the next quarter of the text until the full text is read out. The first reading starts two minutes into the film, the second one two minutes after the end of the first one, and the third and fourth likewise after two-minute intervals. The fourth reading stops two minutes from the end of the film.

At the end of the fourth reading, the man stops pushing and rests leaning forward, his hands on the wardrobe, his head bent down, while breathing heavily. The wardrobe now stands facing the camera with its right side turned slightly toward it exactly as at the beginning of the film and in exactly the same spot. After a while the man turns around, presses his back and head to the side of the wardrobe, his feet out and his eyes looking up. The sequence consists of a series of long and close-up shots, the last one being close-up, showing the man—chest heaving, mouth open and eyes looking up toward the ceiling. The ticking is loud and unpleasant. After some ten seconds the camera moves in a close-up shot to the front of the wardrobe, not showing the man. The door of the wardrobe slowly opens by itself, revealing a large, shiny metal bucket nearly filled with water, more water dripping into it from above into the very center. Waves spread in beautiful rings toward the rim of the bucket from where the water drips. The sound of the dripping drowns out the unpleasant ones, growing gradually louder and louder, in the end sounding beautiful like a church bell.

Long shot from the corner. The man is gone.

Credits appear and run with the view of the wardrobe and the sound of the dripping in the background.

on kicking the bucket

make sur
e you'v
e lost you
r family friend
s they
've lost
you you
they all go
ne no lov
e hard feeling
s left go
ne a blind
spot on the reti
na find a
room a per
fect cub
e emp
ty no door
s windows blind
ing bright white
walls crack
s in them li
ke gian
t crouch
ing spi
ders corners bla
ck smell
y like sweat
y arm
pits crotches a
n aid remind
er why

● ¼
you're the
re a strong brand
new shiny eye
hook in the mid
dle of the cei
ling the ve
ry center a thick
soft gen
tle rope in
it noose on
the end the
knot loos
e sliding a
bucket plas
tic blue gr
een re
d zinc no
matter wha
t strong di
rectly under
neath it top
down wear
a comfort
able sui
t doub
le breast
ed prefer
ably more chest
room with
deep pock
ets black navy
blue navy
● ½

blue preferred l
ess melodra
matic st
and on the buck
et pull
the noose o
ver you
r head a
round you
r neck ma
ke sure it
fits tight
en it feel
its soft
ness kind
ness feel
good stick both
hands in your pock
ets thrust
real deep hold on
to the lin
ing squee
ze squee
ze hard har
d hard
er don't
take a deep
breath ex
hale things will
speed up b
e easie
r close
your eyes jump
up kick

the bucket hear
it fly wai
t for what
's to co
me dark
• ¾
ness don
't fig
ht don
't fig
ht ac
cept it keep
your hand
s in your po
ckets keep th
em closed squee
ze hard hard
hard
er hold on
to the lining in
no case ta
ke them ou
t try grab
bing the noos
e rope en
dure wait you
have no
choice for re
lief to
come it
will it
will in
the end it
will

kaffka's dream

(wild ass)

During rare moments of relaxation before going to bed, after a hard day at the office and hours of writing late into the night, Franz Kaffka (also known as Kafka and even Kaphka because of the ease with which his surname lent itself to misspellings) often fantasized about being an onager—a wild Asian ass. He thought of its body— small and frail-looking, but super strong in reality, its trunk clumsy, shapeless, like a piece of a gnarled tree trunk you couldn't easily split or shape into something, left over as unusable after the smooth parts have been cut off, the spindly legs like match sticks seeming not up to the task of supporting the bulky body above them, the neck short, almost nonexistent, the huge (huge in relation to the rest of the body) head growing practically directly out of the trunk, the only hint about the real strength within for whoever dared to mess with it. (It was no coincidence one of the earliest weapons invented by man, as attested in the Bible, was an ass's jaw attached to a stick—light but durable, capable of inflicting serious damage, a true weapon of mass destruction of its time compared with the unwieldy and unreliable stone ax which could shatter or fly off the handle at the most crucial moment.)

And colors! What could be more beautiful?—The softest of gray along the upper part of the trunk like the gray of the rose would be if roses could be gray, ringed by the pristine white, like that of fresh snow, along the belly, edge of the jaw, and legs.... And speaking of beauty—how about those tiny, shiny, delicate black china cups of hoofs into which the body had been poured?!

Fast as whirlwind (the species is known for its speed) he would race down the flat barren Asian landscape leaving a vortex of red

69

and gray dust behind him like an embodiment of some evil force wanting to catch him but never being able to do it.

At times he would come across a herd—bunch, really, no more than five or six—of female asses guarded by their jealous master-stallion or abandoned by him for a brief while as he dozed off somewhere standing up in the lee of the side of a gully or a bush because of old age or exhaustion from having to satisfy the ever-hungry members of his harem. A fierce battle would ensue in case of the first situation, always ending with his winning decisively while his cowardly opponent ran away at break-neck speed toward the horizon, the bloody wounds from *his* bites all over the latter's body, like fires in pots fanned into flames by wind. The mares would watch the fight calmly, not showing any concern or preference for the combatants, and afterwards would give themselves passively to him, his huge black penis like a well-oiled steel rod in an old-fashioned steam locomotive going in and out of their vaginas.

At times too he would come across a hermit living in a cave—hole—in the side of a gully with a young girl he had managed to dupe into becoming his lover the way the one in Boccaccio's *Decameron* did with the naïve Alibech. He would stand at a distance, or sometimes not so far away, watching the two copulate, hugely aroused, and the girl, seduced by the size of his member, would join him afterwards for more lovemaking, her passion not quenched by the poor underfed holy man, as he lay exhausted either asleep or indifferent to what was happening in the dust on the ground. She would bestow on him the kind of pleasures the ass Lucius received from the Roman or Greek matron (in the state he was in he couldn't remember which) as described by Apuleius in his *Golden Ass.*

He would sit still in the hard, unyielding chair dreaming like this, his hands limp on the table before him, the half-murdered page with the exhausted pen prostrate upon it between them, staring with unfocused eyes into the black Prague night outside the window.

insect people

For Karina

It was a busy day at the office and on coming home Roach Insectly decided to take a little nap on the sofa before fixing himself dinner. He took off his shoes, loosened his tie, unbuttoned the collar of his shirt, put a cushion under his head, lay on his back, stretched out his legs, and closed his eyes. Peace spread through his body coming from somewhere inside it like water from under a rock, gradually carrying away memories of the events of the hectic day. They rose, swayed, bobbed up and down, and slowly floated off somewhere exactly like furniture in a cluttered room filling up with water. He was entering the wonderful hypnogogic state that precedes sleep in which everything is possible when he heard a loud rustling/scratching noise coming from his right. It sounded like a page being turned or better the sound of an insect's legs on paper. Too lazy to expend much energy on finding out what was happening, but his curiosity still aroused, Roach Insectly cracked open his eyelids and looked right without moving his head. He saw large, dark, shiny forms move this way and that by the wall in that direction where a table stood and realized those were huge, human-sized insects, erect, moving on their hind legs. Instantly he became fully awake, reacting to a justifiable sense of fear at what he saw, and his first thought was to jump up and run although he didn't know where. He stopped himself from doing it at the last moment however realizing that since the insects were clearly aware of him and haven't harmed him in any way so far, as long as he stayed still he most likely was safe. Just to make sure however he closed his eyelids as much as possible while still being able to see from under them and proceeded to watch with interest what was happening.

The creatures were a curious bunch indeed! Clearly insects, with their shiny sculpted outer shells, wings, antennae, and faceted eyes, they retained some features of the human body such as legs and feet, arms and hands, cheeks, chins, noses, bellies, behinds, and so on, some many of these, other a few, perhaps only one, and all usually quite deformed. They also wore clothes, except the insect version of the human kind—strange cylindrical or spherical hats, exuberant coats, fancy trousers, bold dresses, provocative skirts, extravagant ties, ingenious shoes, and so on, again some many of these, other a few, perhaps only one.

A peculiar smell hit Roach Insectly's nostrils, a mixture—bundle really—of many strands of scents, some faint, other strong, some pleasant, other harsh, even offensive, and then in an instant he realized what was happening. These were his friends, insect people, like he himself, who had gathered, as they always did on this day of the month, at his place to have dinner together and were letting him rest while they got the food ready. As all insects do they communicated through pheromones and the message he was getting was that everything was alright, progress was being made on the dinner, and he could go on resting until the food was ready. He shifted his gaze onto his chest and saw the shiny black as if covered with Chinese lacquer transverse ribbing of the underside of his body, the tips of the translucent brownish wings with the intricate veining in them like the finest art nouveau stained-glass windows showing at the end, and, he had to admit, the ridiculously feeble-looking afterthought-like legs helplessly sticking up into the air. Pressed against the back of the sofa on his left were visible the folds of the lime-green frock coat he was wearing. He was not looking out from under his eyelids but with a

76

single facet of each of his eyes, the other ones being dormant at this time.

It was always like this—when he was human he had no recollection of his insect life and when he became an insect some time had to pass before the memory of this side of him came back. The same was true of all the others. But it was this life that was the real one. The other one, human, being mere flimsy, transitory moments of no significance in the grander scheme of things.

As he watched his friends preparing the feast his memory was slowly reconstructing itself—there was Dung Bee Tel, the president of the lodge, an ethnic Chinese from Vietnam—or was it Indonesia, Burma, or Thailand?—in human life a restless round little ball of a man like the ball of feces dung beetles push around, in funny striped trousers and a rakishly sliced-off cylinder on his head, running around, making sure things were getting done; Mai Kiefer ("Pine/Jaw" in German), a big, golden creature—a Wagnerian Diva in human life—whose grandfather, she had told him, had changed the family name from Käfer ("Bug"), engrossed in something at the table; Michal Mucha ("Fly"), of Polish origin, wearing an electric-blue cape and enormous wrap-around mirror goggles, preparing drinks, judging from the smell liberally laced with vodka (that is "wódka," as he never failed to point out at the slightest opportunity, doggedly insisting that the drink originated in his home country and not in Russia); the Russian "Zuck" (from "Zhuk" or "Bug") Zhukoffsky, a big, soft blond man, pale to the point of seeming translucent in human life as well as now, carrying in from the kitchen a steaming pot of the salty Russian "piss" ("shchi") soup; Joan Bichejo ("Big Bug") from Spain—Catalonia, really—with his pencil-thin mustache having turned into a pair of magnificent, luxuriant antennae Salvador Dali would have been envious of, fixing the insect equivalent of *tapas*; Ray ("P. Raymond") Mantis, nearly seven feet tall, knock-kneed and loose-jointed in human life, tossing a gigantic salad, his extraordinarily long and thin front legs pressed together at the knees; and all the others, making rustling and crunching noises at the table and running this way and that.

Roach Insectly remembered his human life. How primitive it was compared to his life as an insect! It was like comparing his childhood years to his life as an adult. The constant futile groping for truth, the misunderstandings and misrepresentations of facts!... Just a few days ago for instance, while in his insect state, he saw a scene from nearly two thousand years ago and it was completely different from what is commonly assumed to have been like. It was the crucifixion of Christ or rather his walking to the place he was going to be crucified. It went as follows.

There was a vast plane stretching as far as the eye could see to the left and right going up at an angle of about fifteen degrees to the sky. It was perfectly flat and smooth as if made from one sheet of plywood and painted a shiny bright red. The sky was a deep blue and without a single cloud in it. In the middle of the plane, moving up it, a man was carrying a cross. It was Christ. His flesh was green and the hair long and reddish brown. A scraggy sparse beard of the same color as the hair framed his face. He was naked except for a dirty white loincloth wrapped around his middle and a crown of thorns made from forged iron on top of his head. The cross was big and white, made from freshly-cut wood, still wet and therefore obviously very heavy. It rested on Christ's left shoulder, one of its arms going down along his chest. Christ held onto it with both hands, clutching it desperately, afraid it would fall down. The end of the cross dragged on the ground. Christ moved in quick short steps trying in vain to dig his feet into the hard surface and moving from side to side in order to ease his task. Because of the exertion sweat stood out on his face and even torso in big drops, rolling down them onto the plane. It wasn't green but clear, unnaturally so, and magnified the skin beneath it like liquid lenses. You could see the black pores under it, the network of lines connecting these, and the short dark hair timidly clinging to the skin as if afraid.

Suddenly a girl appeared at the top of the plane a little to the right of the center and proceeded to run toward Christ. She was tall and slender, with short, blond, wavy hair, an attractive chiseled face, and green eyes, and was dressed in a long white gown. The hair and the gown swung gaily as she ran as if in anticipation of what would happen and the open mouth, distended as if in a smile, showed two rows of beautiful, even, pearl-white teeth. On reaching Christ the girl grabbed his neck and shook him violently as if trying to wake him up from deep sleep. Christ stopped as this happened but showed no attempt at resisting the girl. The girl shook Christ a few more times and then, her face made hideous by hatred and determination, proceeded to claw Christ's face with her fingernails. She would dig them deeply into his flesh, mostly along the forehead and cheeks, and tear it with them, leaving long wide gashes running with blood. The blood ran down Christ's face saturating his beard and dripping off it onto his torso and the plane. As he had done when the girl shook him by the neck Christ showed no attempt at resisting the girl, enduring the torture stoically for a while but then suddenly he apparently couldn't take it any longer, his body shook as if retching, he toppled over to the left, and fell down with the cross, landing on top of it and remaining to lie there on his left side in the fetal position his feet drawn up, stiff and still like a very old person afraid or unable to move. When Christ fell down the girl didn't squat down and continue torturing him as one would have expected but remained standing over him still, her arms sticking stiffly away from her body as if afraid they would stain her gown. They were covered with blood and it dripped off her fingers onto the plane. The tips of the latter looked ragged from the flesh and skin sticking out from under the nails.

As soon as Christ fell down a man appeared at the bottom of the plane a little to the left of the center and proceeded to run at full speed toward Christ. He was dressed in a long gown like the girl except it wasn't as white but closer to beige. To ease his running he held up the edge of his gown with his left hand on the level of his knees. While this was happening Christ rolled over to his right almost onto his back, stretched his legs out, and remained lying in this position breathing heavily, trying to regain his strength. On reaching Christ the man bent down and tried to lift the cross off the plane by its free left arm. At first he had a hard time doing it, the cross slipping out of his hands, but eventually he was able to raise it off the ground and then higher and higher. As this happened Christ's body started to slide off the cross and realizing what was happening he rolled off it, got onto his knees, and straightened up. By then the man had raised the cross to a vertical position, with its right arm resting on the plane. Christ put his left shoulder in the nook formed by the two beams and started to get up. Seeing this the man got down on his right knee right behind Christ while still holding onto the cross with his left hand, put his right shoulder under the beam, and proceeded to get up together with Christ. With both of them lifting they raised the cross without much trouble. Once on his feet Christ proceeded carrying the cross up the plane as before. The man then got out from under the beam but continued walking on Christ's left, from time to time putting his right hand on the cross, making sure it wouldn't slip off Christ's shoulder. Christ moved hesitatingly at first, reeling from side to side as if drunk, but after a few steps steadied himself and proceeded to walk as before he fell down. The girl walked along with the two men on their right, her hands still sticking stiffly away from her body as if starched. The trio reached the top of the plane and disappeared there. From the way they did this it was clear it ended in a flat platform at the top. It must have been Golgotha.

As soon as the three figures vanished from sight a huge crowd of people appeared at the bottom of the plane from one end of it to the other and proceeded to run up it as the man had done, screaming loudly and shaking their fists. They were men, women, and children all dressed as the man and the girl were in long gowns, except not only white but also of other colors, mostly faded gray, brown, red, and blue. Some of them held up their gowns as the man had done. Some of them again—mostly men—also carried sticks or clubs in their hands which they brandished furiously. On reaching the top of the plane the people disappeared there as the trio had done. More people kept appearing at the bottom however so that the plane was a vast waterfall of humanity moving up the plane and spilling over it at the top.

At first Roach Insectly didn't understand the meaning of what he saw but then realized that the woman was Mary Magdalene who was also Veronica. She helped Christ suffer. The man was Simon of Cyrene. And the crowd were the people of Jerusalem or more likely of all of Palestine. At first again he couldn't figure out who they were angry at—the people responsible for what was happening to Christ or Christ himself—but then realized that it was both—the two angers were the same.

Roach Insectly recalled next the endless days of despair especially in late March when a person's life élan has been drained away by the interminable harsh winter and spring hasn't yet announced definitively its return, snow having merely receded in places on the slopes of hills like flesh on the thigh of a corpse, with either him or someone else—he wasn't sure who—pacing the dirty worn floors in the bleak unheated railcar-type apartment, sometimes actually running from room to room as if looking for someone, or

81

for hours on end writhing in agony on the narrow hard sofa, unsure of whether or not God existed. "Unsure of whether or not god existed...." How can you be unsure of whether or not someone exists when you are sitting in the person's bright and cozy kitchen with him/her across the able smiling warmly at you while affectionately squeezing your hand? And people get proofs of God's existence every second of every minute of every day except are unable to understand them with their primitive human minds. Take for instance the following that happened once, again either to him or to some other man—once more he wasn't sure who.

He (that is either he or the man in question) had been suspecting a woman he was in love with of being unfaithful to him. One day, unable to stand the uncertainty any longer, he followed her through the city streets as she hurried somewhere, nervously glancing over her shoulder from time to time, obviously afraid of being tailed. At first he had no idea where she was going but then with a sinking heart realized his worst fears were coming true and that she was headed for the red-light district of town. He hoped this wasn't true, that she was merely going to skirt it on her way to her destination, but she was headed for the very heart of it! Weak in the knees, his heart pounding wildly in his chest, he marshaled all the strength he could muster to keep up with her as she hurried through the narrow, twisted streets, staying at a safe distance behind her so as not to be detected.

There was a place he knew which was the very essence of depravity—a whorehouse frequented by drug addicts, beggars, and homeless men, the lowest of the low, and that is where she seemed to be headed. Every turn she took and every step she made brought her closer and closer to it and with each of them his hopes that she was going someplace else diminished. Finally they were in the street the place was on. It was on the other side of the street from them. She crossed the street cutting through it at

82

an angle and headed straight for the door. There was no doubt now she was going there. The whorehouse was situated in the basement of a building and there were steps leading from the sidewalk down to its door. She stepped off the sidewalk and proceeded down the steps. Little by little the lower part of her body disappeared under the ground as if swallowed up by it. The sidewalk really seemed to be devouring her from her feet up. She had sunken down to her neck and only her head covered by the beautifully molded blond hair was still visible. Suddenly she turned her head so that he could see her face. It was turned up and her mouth opened in a smile. Far as it was he realized with horror that her teeth weren't perfectly white as he had always thought but black in places, especially where they joined, rotted away as in people suffering from some horrible venereal disease. This was the last straw and he accepted it. Now he was ready for anything. Her lips moved and he realized that a man was walking along the sidewalk past her at that moment and that she was speaking to him. He must have said something to her and she was answering him back. Given the context there was little doubt that what he had said was something indecent and she had taken it as a compliment. The man passed her, she turned her head back and proceeded down the steps. In a couple of seconds her head disappeared under the sidewalk. He saw the door open and close and knew she had gone inside.

He had no control over his actions. Like a moth drawn to a light he also headed for the place. He didn't know what he would do there but felt he had to go inside. He reached the steps and continued down them. He had descended almost to the bottom when the door opened and people started coming out of it. They carried long, light objects, that turned out to be lily stalks and stiff, naked corpses. Some of the lilies were wilted, other completely dried out, still other fresh, succulent, with drops of dew-like water on them. The corpses were completely dried out because the

83

people carried them with no effort as if they were lilies. The people climbed the steps up to the street and he had to stop and press his back to the wall to let them pass. They were forced to squeeze past him, brushing against his body, the lilies and corpses touching his hands and wetting them as if with drops of dew. He stood patiently waiting for the precession to end. But the people kept coming. There were dozens of them, perhaps more... more than a hundred.... It seemed comical like a scene out of a silent movie with an endless row of people coming out of a car. But finally the procession stopped. He saw the last person disappear at the top of the steps. It was time for him to move on, to go through with his painful task. Reluctantly he turned, descended the steps to the very bottom, opened the door, and stepped inside.

What should have awaited him there was either her waiting in the reception room for a customer, he being potentially one, her going with a customer down a narrow passageway to one of the cubicles, or her already being inside one of the cubicles with a customer and another woman or women waiting for a customer, he being potentially one. But what he found was something completely different. He had come to a place where he was going to be given a proof of the existence of God.

There was an immaculate whiteness all around and bright but unobtrusive light, and the feeling of a warm smile across a table from him, and someone affectionately squeezing his hand. He was given a sheet of paper on which the proof of God's existence was presented as that of a mathematical theorem. It was short—only a few brief paragraphs—and written in a strange alphabet and a language neither of which he knew, but as he looked at it he followed it completely. The meaning behind every symbol, word, phrase, sentence, paragraph, entered his consciousness directly without going through the process of translation. He absorbed it fully, not losing the slightest implication of it and in the process

84

seemed to grow in size, was amazed at his growth, and wondered where it would stop. It was as if a vast Gothic cathedral were being built within and around him with the sound of a mighty organ playing in it. He was amazed at the size and beauty of the first and the power and magnificence of the second and suddenly saw her in the center of the cathedral by the altar standing still, dressed in white, her eyes closed, a beatific smile on her lips and her arms meekly crossed on her chest.

But this never registered in his or the man's consciousness as if he or the man were in a state of coma and their mind couldn't record it. The proof had been given in vain, to someone who would never be able to appreciate it, put it to good use. What a waste!

And now as he lay on the sofa Roach Insectly saw the final scene of his life which he would not see the same way as a human. It went as follows.

He is rushing along the landing at the top of the stairs of a church toward its door, about to enter it. It towers tall with its pointed arch before him. He is dressed in a black-tie outfit—is going in to get married to a woman he has searched for all his life. It will be a totally happy marriage which will last till his death. His bride already waits for him inside.

He enters the church. It is big, dark, and empty. An organ is playing. Up ahead is the altar and a group of people are gathered in a little crowd beside it. Among them is a slender figure in white— she! He smiles internally and walks quickly down the aisle toward her. She grows bigger and bigger with his every step and finally he is near her. He has never seen her before and has not thought about what she should look like but realizes she looks exactly as he had expected—her features had existed in his subconscious and have risen to the surface now. She is beautiful in a gentle, quiet way the way a glass of clear water is clear and the way it tastes delicious without ostensibly having any taste. Her face is covered with a veil. He raises it and their lips touch. He is replaced by their softness and moisture. It is a foretaste of her core. He couldn't feel any happier. The goal of his life has been achieved! He opens his eyes and sees her eyes glitter close to him like a crystal chandelier. His feeling of happiness is reinforced but for some reason he has an urge to turn around. Not far away, still in front of the altar, he sees a table with a coffin on top of it. The lid of the coffin is open and you can see its inside upholstered with black velvet. The outside of the coffin is white. A man dressed in black is leaning a ladder to the side of the table. He realizes it is for him. He has to step into the coffin. There is no sadness in him however—it is part of the ceremony he is going through, his wedding. He turns away from his bride, walks to the table, and climbs the ladder. The man takes his hand, making sure he won't fall down. He gets up on the table, steps inside the coffin, sits down, and lowers himself so as to lie down on his back. Before doing this however he rests on his elbow and looks in the direction of the group of people with whom his bride is. They stand there huddled together, smiling and waving to him. Some of them hold bouquets of white flowers. Then he hears a noise from the other side and turns his head in that direction. The man who had helped him into the coffin has climbed a few steps up the ladder and is standing with a bottle of champagne raised in his hand. He smashes it on the side of the coffin and it breaks, exploding with black foam. The champagne was black. He is pleased by what he sees—the ceremony is beautiful and is progressing as it should.

He turns his head back to the group of people and waves with his free hand to them. They wave back to him. He feels an unsteady sensation and realizes the coffin is sailing off. The people seem to sway as if liquid themselves. Everything he sees sways too as if having turned to liquid. It is as if only he remained solid. He is happy. He is setting out on a joyous journey which is to be like a honeymoon except it will last forever. He feels he has been lucky—not everyone achieves in life what he has achieved, namely to be where he is. He casts one more look at the people. His bride is among the people but they all have actually merged into one. It is as if they were one big, important person. He makes one last wave with his hand, turns around, lies down, crosses his hands on his chest, and closes his eyes. A sharp, loud bang is heard—the lid of the coffin has closed down on him.

What Roach Insectly saw had profound and far-reaching implications but he realized with sadness that he wouldn't remember even the slightest intimation of it in his human life. He thought about Kafka. Genius that he was he intuitively sensed the truth about people when he wrote his "Metamorphosis" but in the end was unable to break through to its core. Had he done so the world might have been a happier place now.

Peace had returned to Roach Insectly and he again felt himself drifting off into sleep. His sensors stimulated by the pheromones that were wafting his way told him he still had some time before dinner was ready so he decided to let himself nap. He turned off the two functioning facets in his eyes and entered a delicious darkness.

banana moon over cancun

1.

A banana, Rogerio Navas smiled inwardly, catching a glimpse of the huge sickle moon in the clear silvery sky through the opening between the palm tree tops and the wall of tall reeds beyond which he knew shimmered the still Cancun bay. The taste of the banana or bananas—he didn't bother to try ascertaining which—he had consumed a little while back was still fresh in his mouth and was undoubtedly at least partly responsible for the image arising in his mind. The moon was a few days past being new and its middle looked thick, just like a fat banana. A few days more and it would bulge like the belly of a pregnant woman starting to show— Carmen growing big with his child.

Rogerio Navas smiled again, this time outwardly, and for a second closed his eyes from the pleasure brought on by the reality of the situation. He was almost by the bench where they had said they would meet and, being almost as punctual as he unlike the vast majority of women, in a few minutes she would be there. He had glanced at his watch just a little while back and he was then five minutes early. Carmen was walking from the direction of the strip where she was attending a meeting in one of the hotels closest to town, which was within walking distance of the spot, and should be there on time.

In a few strides he was beyond the bend the path made running along the wall of reeds in this part of the walk and saw the bench sheltering timidly in the darkness, not reached by the light of the street lamp by the side of the road some ten yards away, perched like a seagull on the arm sticking away from the top of the slender aluminum post.

Rogerio Navas stepped off the concrete path, went up to the bench, sat down, and mechanically glanced at his watch—it was two minutes to nine. Soon she would be with him. He looked left to see if she was coming down the path but there was no one there. The light seemed a slender female figure standing by the lamp post, waiting for a bus that was scheduled to arrive any minute. Rogerio Navas leaned against the back rest, spread his arms out along it, and crossed his right leg over the left one.

He and Carmen had known each other for over four months, since she came to him with her husband to discuss the matter of artificial insemination. The two had been married for five years, she couldn't get pregnant, and it had just been established the husband was the cause. They were referred to him by their doctor, he being the artificial insemination specialist in town. The moment Rogerio Navas saw her he realized this wasn't going to be a simple professional relationship. There was a chasm between her and her husband that apparently only the latter couldn't see—he an accountant, in a dark suit, conservative tie, starched white shirt with gold cufflinks, gold-rimmed glasses, his black hair slicked down, handsome in a nineteen-thirties way but clearly regimented like a clock mechanism inside its case; she flashing an unbelievable beauty and sexual magnetism like a huge Turkish scimitar, not bothering to hide her attraction to him so that he made no attempt to hide his, sure the man would not notice it with his bookkeeper's mind capable of dealing only with numbers arranged in columns and rows.

Two weeks later, when it was the optimum time for her to get pregnant, he inseminated her with two cubic centimeters of his semen collected in a paroxysm of solitary ecstasy that morning, produced during a week of carefully guarded abstinence and used instead of the sample selected by her and her husband from the sperm bank in his office. A few drops of her husband's empty semen had been added to it in a silly gesture aimed more at placating the hypocrisy of the society than her husband's masculine ego. A week later they made love for the first time on the cold hard floor in his examining room and three weeks later she was pregnant.

It was only a matter of time when the truth would be revealed to everyone—they merely hadn't decided whether it should be before or after the birth of the baby. He couldn't bear the thought of her husband lying in bed next to her every night even though she assured him that whatever happened between them in bed left her completely cold.

A sound of footsteps reached Rogerio Navas' ears coming from behind the wall of reeds hiding the path on the left. It's Carmen, he thought and again smiling inwardly started to get up so as to greet her. But at that instant the figure of an Indian man with a stocky square body and short legs emerged from behind the edge of the wall of the reeds and his tensed-up muscles relaxed. It was one of the hotel workers hurrying home. The man took no notice of Rogerio Navas as if too discrete to look in his direction and in a matter of seconds disappeared behind the wall of reeds on the right. Soon he would be having supper with his wife and kids.

Rogerio Navas glanced at his watch. It was ten after nine—strange that Carmen hadn't come yet. He again observed she was very punctual as a rule but explained to himself the meeting must have run late and she was unable to get away on time. But it couldn't go on much longer, so very soon she was bound to be there. He calmed down and continued to wait. But impatience, one of his bothersome traits, started gnawing on his mind, making him uncomfortable sitting down. He got up and began pacing back and forth along the path in front of the bench, every few seconds stopping and turning his ear in the direction of the hotels to hear if she was coming. The path however continued still as if the space in that direction had been filled with concrete. At one point a bus came driving down the empty road from the direction of the hotels, all lit up inside and full of people—workers returning home from their jobs. This calmed Rogerio Navas down—there was life where the bus came from and Carmen was part of it. He glanced at his watch. It was twenty after nine. She should be there any minute. He concluded it was really surprising however that she still hadn't come. The meeting couldn't have dragged on that long and if it did she would have excused herself knowing how he would feel waiting for her on the bench. Something out of the ordinary must have happened. He only hoped it was nothing serious. But what serious could have happened to her? The last hotel was just a short distance away and the reeds didn't run along the path except for a short stretch in the spot where he was. She must have just gotten held up for a reason he couldn't imagine. She would come any minute, her absence would be explained, and everything would return to normal. Once again his worries went away but the impatience returned. His fingers twisted as if belonging to someone else and resisted him stubbornly as he was trying to hold them still.

Another bus, almost empty, with one or two passengers in it, drove in the other direction. Rogerio Navas glanced at his watch again. It was twenty-five after... twenty-five after ten, not after nine! He turned cold and then hot, felt sweat stand out on his face and neck. Somehow, he'd been misreading his watch and was an hour late! Carmen came, waited for him, and went home.

He calmed down somewhat but the guilt for his mistake pushed its way out into the open. How could he have done something so stupid as misreading his watch by an hour? He turned away from the direction of the hotels and faced the bench. Next to one end of it on the ground he noticed for the first time the peels of what looked like two bananas. Something stirred in his memory—had he dropped them there? He thought he recalled sitting in that spot and eating a banana while he waited for her. But he hadn't done it just now, he was sure of that. Was he there once before that evening? It didn't make sense. He concluded he was either just imagining it or that it was a memory out of his past, probably from another bench.   Bananas were his favorite fruit and he had consumed a lot of them in his lifetime. The explanation didn't satisfy him however. The recollection of his sitting very recently on the bench and eating a banana while waiting for Carmen was too vivid in his mind to be just a thought. And then what had he been doing for an hour while waiting for Carmen? He was sure he left his office at eight thirty, having worked late so as to catch up with an avalanche of work, and planned to go straight to the spot where he was to meet Carmen.   He was certain of the time because he had talked about it with his assistant who stayed on in the office after him. What had he done for an extra hour? The skin on his skull and nape of his neck grew numb and a wave of confusion rolled over him. He couldn't remember what he had been doing! He rubbed his face with his hand—it felt greasy with sweat like a frying pan and the sensation disgusted him. He felt sick. There was something wrong with him. Had he had a spell of amnesia?

Hoping to help himself resolve the issue of the missing hour, although not knowing how this would help, he walked up to the bench and picked up the banana peel—it was only one, with the stub of another one attached to it. It hung limp in his fingers, unable to help him in any way.

Realizing he could place no blame on the banana, Rogerio Navas lifted his eyes and looked at the wall of reeds before him. It was some six feet away from the bench. Above it he could see with the corner of his eye the sickle moon, now smaller and no longer looking like a banana, indifferent to what was happening down below, hanging free in the empty sky.

The reeds stood straight and thick along the edge except in one spot, close to the right end of the bench where there was a parting in them and a few broken stalks. Someone most likely had pushed their way through them to get inside the thicket recently. Rogerio Navas recalled he and Carmen going in there once early in their affair and making love on the ground, unable to control their passion for each other that had rolled over them like a crashing sea wave.

Rogerio Navas' heart sank and started pounding violently. He hadn't yet formulated the situation he was afraid of but knew it had something to do with Carmen being harmed. His arms trembling, the limp banana peel swinging in his fingers, he went up to the parting and pushing the reeds apart stepped in among them, feeling he was willingly getting himself into a situation that would bring him no good.

Some six feet into the thicket there was a clearing in the reeds where he and Carmen had made love that time long ago. As he parted the last stalks that separated him from the spot he saw in the darkness something formless lying on the ground, mostly pale but also white and black. His heart sank again and a faint cry like a frightened bird rose up in his chest, entered his throat, and pushed its way out through his mouth. He rushed forward and fell on his knees, seeing that it was the body of a woman lying on her back, spread-eagled, her skirt pulled up, naked from the waist down. A small shapeless white object lay next to her, a few feet

96

away—clearly her panties. The modishly short black hair, the elegantly curved eyebrows, the delicate nose were familiar and so dear to him! Above the big black triangle of the pubis curved the still barely bulging but already undeniably pregnant belly.

Carmen! Oh, my God! Rogerio Navas shouted, dropping the banana peel from his hand and grabbing the body by the shoulders but recoiled instantly, put off, as if frightened, by its limpness. There was no doubt she was dead.

And then Rogerio Navas noticed—admitted to seeing—something strange and truly disgusting—a weird formless shape sticking out of her mouth, obscuring part of her cheekbone and lower jaw. He looked at it closely and realized it was a banana, unpeeled, which had been shoved into her mouth, apparently to stifle her cries. It may have choked her.

Horror overcame Rogerio Navas. Different thoughts flashed through his mind concerning what might have happened to Carmen. For a few seconds he couldn't arrange them into anything coherent but then the following scenarios formed themselves in his mind.

Carmen had been killed while being raped. While she was waiting for him she was approached by someone, forced into the reeds, made to undress partly, raped, and then killed. Who could it have been? A worker going home from his job? Not likely. Her husband? Perhaps. He may have found out what was happening between him and her, had stalked her, and while she was waiting for him, approached her, forced her into the reeds, and committed the crime. If this was so, the man could be waiting for him now, hiding in the reeds. Chills ran up Rogerio Navas' spine and, still on his knees, he turned around quickly as if hearing the reeds rustle behind his back while someone was pushing his way out of them. But there was no one there.

But that was unlikely, Rogerio Navas thought, relaxing. The man wouldn't have waited for him for an hour. He probably wouldn't have waited at all but would have run away from the scene of the crime right away so as not to be caught.

But that scenario didn't seem very convincing to Rogerio Navas anyway. There were too many elements in it that didn't fit. Carmen wasn't with him so how would her husband know she was meeting him? And why would he want to rape her if he could have her in bed that night? And then there was the banana in Carmen's mouth—why would he have carried it with him? And why would anyone ready to commit a murder carry a banana with him anyway? This reminded him of the taste of a freshly consumed banana in his mouth—he had an instinctive feeling it had something to do with the murder. Did he kill Carmen? He grew numb at the thought. Again, he had a distinct feeling he had sat on the bench that night eating a banana. According to the peel he had picked up there were two bananas joined at the stalk—he ate one and the other one he must have stuffed in her mouth. But why would he have killed her? They loved each other passionately. But maybe she had some bad news for him—wanted to tell him she had decided to stick with her husband and not see him anymore. He remembered with horror it was she who had suggested they meet by the bench so that they could take a walk into town and talk. He had thought the motivation was something romantic but perhaps it was something else. But then she would have given him the bad news while they were walking and not right by the bench. The whole thing didn't make sense. He was confused again. Thoughts circulated through his mind like things in a pot of boiling water and the only thing he was sure of was that he couldn't account for an hour of his time that evening. He felt it had something to do with Carmen's death.

And then the reality of the situation hit him for the first time. Carmen was dead and he would never see her alive again! And the baby was dead too! The idyllic life they had been planning together would never come to pass. It would forever remain just words which were incapable of turning into reality. His future seemed an endless empty plain. The prospect of his living was unbearable.

In despair he raised his eyes and looked at the sky. The moon was now merely a painfully bright, cold, sickle-shaped form in a vast empty space that had no relationship to the agony he was going through down below. And he was the cause of this agony. How could he have killed Carmen? He was not a human being but an animal, a monster! .... A howl of anguish pushed this time its way from his chest up to his lips, parted them, and rushed out into the open. He thought he sounded like a wolf howling at the moon and then felt this is exactly what he was.

At that instant he heard a voice what seemed right next to him but which he assumed came from somewhere outside the reeds on the path in reality. He grew numb with fear again and instantly fell flat on the ground, pressing his body as close to it as possible, just as he used to press it against his mother's bosom as a little boy when he would run to her and fall into her arms, crying when something bad had happened to him. With all his might he hoped he hadn't been heard by whoever was there. The voice sounded again, this time seemingly farther away, on the background of the sound of rhythmic footsteps—there were actually two of them, clearly a pair of workers chatting while walking down the path on their way back into town. The sounds grew progressively fainter. Soon they would be gone. He was safe. His howl had not been heard. He couldn't help noticing with a sense of horror however that his left hand was right next to his head—he had laid it there so as not to touch Carmen's body.

2.

The "RA-ta-ta, RA-ta-ta" racket that had permeated every cell of his body suddenly stopped, as if deciding it would never be able to catch the train it had been pursuing for so long and scurrying back into the tunnel where it felt safe. The train emerged from under the ground and sped nimbly and nearly silently down the tracks into the urban landscape before it. Roger stirred in his seat. Enough daydreaming, time to return to reality!   He glanced instinctively to his left to look for the moon but his eyes were met with the huge reddish-gray cubes of the brick tenement buildings that ran along this portion of the track almost next to it. In the gaps between them, way in the distance, could be seen strips of a charcoal-gray sky which looked sooty even while dark. If the moon were to be seen, he thought, it wouldn't be much to look at anyway, not in these surroundings. But it was probably still too early for it to be out. Maybe it would be out when he got home.... And there it probably wouldn't look too bad.

But where was his home? His heart sank as he realized he didn't remember. He knew the stations the train would be stopping at but didn't know which one he should get off at, what kind of home he was coming to, whether or not someone would be meeting him there, and if someone were who the person would be. Instantly his face and neck got wet with sweat and he felt hot and cold all over. What was his name? It was on the tip of his tongue but he couldn't get it out.... No, it wasn't. He had no idea what his name was! Now he felt extremely hot as if a great fire raged inside him. He sat up, gulped, and ran his finger around the collar of his shirt to loosen it up a little. It was choking him. He was afraid to move

100

and even look around lest any action cause more damage to his already seriously damaged self. What was he to do?

He remembered his wallet and the id's he carried in them. He could get it out and find out what his name was and where he lived. He was about to do it when he realized this might not help. What if the id's he carried were not his but another person's? The name, the address, the pictures might be those of a total stranger, someone he had never seen before.... The more he thought about it the more he was sure this is what would happen. The prospect was terrifying. What should he do? Sweat ran in rivulets down his face and he felt it hang in drops off his chin and nose. He had never sweated like this before. He was afraid people would notice it and say something. Quickly he put his hand in his pocket, got out his handkerchief, and dried his face and neck. Then he put the handkerchief back in the pocket. He felt better for a few seconds but then the worries returned. He was sure now the picture on the driver's license in the wallet was that of a fat, pale, man with thinning blond hair, combed back straight, looking like a pig. He had no idea who the man was but felt a strong loathing toward him and wanted to be as far away from him as possible. He thought of moving away on his seat but realized this wouldn't help.

For a while he remained still. The rhythmic motion of the train transferred to his body which swayed in harmony with its surroundings and some peace returned to him. But the picture on the driver's license in his wallet kept coming back to his mind. He wanted to see it, to see if it really was that of the pale, fat man that looked like a pig. Perhaps he was wrong. Perhaps the id's in his wallet were his, he would find out who he was, everything would come back to normal, and he would continue on his way home. Then he could forget about this silly incident and return to the life he had led until then. But on the other hand he was afraid his original suspicion would be confirmed and then he didn't know what he would do. He didn't want to face that. He struggled with himself as if with another man in a fight until death. Every few seconds he would bend forward, reach for his wallet, but at the last instant would stop himself, afraid to face the truth. In the end he couldn't hold himself back however and so he stuck his hand in his pocket, got the wallet, took it out, opened it, and looked at the driver's license inside it. His heart pounded so wildly in his chest it seemed it was up in his throat.

The picture was that of a dark-haired man with a not unattractive, youthful face. Instinctively he glanced to his left and looked in the reflection in the window. What he saw was a reasonable similarity to the picture in the wallet. He breathed a sigh of relief. He was himself! He looked at the driver's license again and recognized his name and address. With it a whole flood of information rushed in on him—the memories of his entire life—and he felt himself float comfortably in it as in warm water filling a huge bathtub.

He knew now what lay ahead. He would get off at a particular station and walk to his house which was a short distance away. If the moon was out and it was close to full, he would see it sharp and jagged like a cut out end of a tin can through the wispy branches of the pine trees along the driveway as he would walk up it toward the dark house. When he would open the door and step inside before turning on the light, the darkness in the corner would be like a tall figure dressed in a long black cape hiding behind it. Chills would run up his spine as he would realize it was holding a long sharp knife in its hand which it was planning to bury in his side.

Roger returned to his surroundings. People sat in their seats swaying to the rhythm of the motion of the train like heavy bundles in precarious positions threatening to topple over. An ad

102

on the wall before of him, black on white, reminded him of a chart in an optometrist's office, the letters on each successive line getting smaller and smaller until they couldn't be read.

son

a mininovel

1. an egg

After fidgeting around in the armchair and squirming in her underclothes for a while Mary felt something round and big come out of her vagina and settle in her crotch. She thought it was her period finally coming after an unusually long delay and because of being heavy feeling like that, but when she stuck her hand in her panties and felt between her legs she discovered it was a smooth hard object shaped like an egg. She pulled the thing out and saw to her amazement that it was in fact an egg—perfectly white and oval, exactly like a normal chicken egg if perhaps a bit bigger than what you would normally get in a grocery store.

It was warm and although it had come out of her felt practically dry, nestling snugly in her hand like a little animal that had made itself comfortable there and was not planning to leave.

Where did it come from? She was sure she didn't stick it inside her and there was no chance of someone else having done it. This meant she had laid it herself! It was bizarre! She had never heard of a woman—a human being—laying a chicken egg. How could it have happened? Were there chicken genes mixed in with her human ones inside her? She worked at a poultry processing plant and was it possible that they had somehow gotten into her body from her handling chicken carcasses with bare hands all day long day after day? Or did she inherit them from her parents? — Her last name was "Henley," which she got from her father and which hinted at a connection to chickens, but her mother's family name was also "Henley," although her parents weren't related, and she got a double dose of whatever chicken connection the name might carry. So that may have been the reason behind her laying the egg. But be it as it may, why would she lay one all of a sudden?

And then she remembered the incident with a stranger at a party about a month earlier. They had gone into a dark room and he had made love to her on top of the coats piled up on the bed. It happened, she realized now, at about the time when she was ovulating. Yes, that must be the reason for her laying the egg! She recalled further as she thought on that the man had come in with a long red-and-yellow rooster feather stuck in his hat, that he had strutted around proudly in a jerky fashion like a rooster among the guests, and that there were yellow concentric circles in his brown, perfectly round, unblinking eyes like those of a chicken. She must have intuitively sensed he carried chicken genes the same as she and was attracted to him because of that. And he likewise must have noticed the effect of the chicken genes in her— her placid nature for instance— and was attracted to her as a result. And since they both had chicken genes inside them, when he impregnated her, what came out was not a baby but an egg.

They had gone off to the room without saying a word to each other or communicating through some special gesture, and after it was over, he slid off her just like a rooster after mounting a hen and walked out of the room without saying anything. And after fixing herself up she followed him unoffended, just as a hen would after having been mounted, and they stayed away from each other for as long as he was there as if nothing had transpired between them.

He left the party not too long after she came out and she'd heard someone comment at about that time that he was Hungarian and had served in the Royal Gendarmes, which were famous for wearing hats that had rooster feathers in them, and that that must have been the reason why he had one stuck in his, but learned

108

nothing else about him. So, she didn't even know his name. But what was she to do with the egg? Should she throw it away? Out the window? She shuddered at the thought of seeing it smashed on the sidewalk below, the yellow yolk spreading among the white fragments of the shell. Cook it? Put it in boiling water or fry it in a pan... fried or scrambled? And then eat it? What horror! She would be a cannibal, a mother eating her own child!

A child! Of course. That's what it essentially was, if not quite completed. What remained was for it to hatch. And if she was the mother it was her obligation to insure it. This could be achieved by incubating it. She could put it in a box on top of a towel and have it stay under a lamp, as is sometimes done in labs or other places, when she was at work or busy with things and warm it with her body when she was able to. And she could definitely do it while in bed, although she would have to make sure she didn't crush it in her sleep. Since she was the mother, it would be a pleasure for her to do it.

She wondered what would eventually come out of the egg. A tiny little baby or a chick? It didn't matter. Whatever came out would be her child.

She decided she would hatch the egg.

2. chanti

What came out of the egg was of course a chick—a ball of yellow fluff on two pin-thin legs that would chirp testily and refuse to budge as you tried to push it with your finger. At the beginning it stayed mostly in the shoe box which she'd padded with an old terry cloth towel, under a lamp, and then was permitted to roam around first in the kitchen and later throughout the kitchen and the rest of her one-room apartment.

109

It fed on grain and seeds and drank water from a saucer which it would peck as if it was able to see in the liquid the drop it was about to consume like a kernel of grain.

You couldn't tell its sex at first but as its spherical shape became replaced by an oblong one with an upward projection up front, it proceeded to develop signs which made its gender undeniable. It had a distinct crest growing on top of its head and strutted around proudly as if it was too good for its surroundings—it was a rooster.

She named him "Alexander" after her late father but eventually referred to him as "Chanti," derived from the French "*Chanticler*," name for a rooster, derived in turn from "*chanter*," "to sing," and "*cler*," "clear," because of the strong crystal-clear voice with which he announced himself at dawn and on and off throughout the day when so desiring as he grew mature.

Full-grown, he was a magnificent specimen of male *Gallus gallus domesticus*, with a big shocking-pink comb and wattle, a mantle of golden and golden-brown plumage over the upper part of his body, plum-black tending to gray covering over the lower rest of it down to the legs, and an exuberant sheaf of long shiny black feathers for a tail that swayed proudly this way and that as he walked. He had his father's unusual concentric unblinking eyes and moved in the same jerky, stuttering fashion.

3. in the park

Sundays during those times were meant for parks which were huge, stretching flat on all sides to the horizon, so that the houses that stood there looked tiny, barely distinguishable from the grass and inexplicably smaller than the figures of the people—the size of giant ants moving clumsily on their hind legs—that walked past them.

The weather was beautiful, sunny and warm, with a pale blue cloudless sky, and in the afternoon Mary took her son to a park she liked which was on the other side of town.

She spread out the blanket which she'd brought along on the hard ground, tied one of Chanti's legs to hers with a twine, stretched out on her side so as to make it easier for him to move around, and supporting herself clumsily on one arm watched what was going on.

The field with its short grass must have been recently ironed with a huge tailor's iron for it looked like a giant table covered with a smooth green cloth without a crease in it. Someone was flying an enormous pale blue kite way up high in the sky which hid it completely but miraculously was letting the sun shine through as if it wasn't there.

Not far away boys were playing baseball and you could hear their shrill voices breaking the silence, punctuated by the occasional sharp crack of a bat hitting the ball.

Chanti found the game interesting because he kept straining, pulling her leg in the direction where the game was played so that Mary was forced to pull him back over and over again.

At one point one of the batters hit a spectacular home run and the ball kept rolling when it hit the ground, resting only a few feet away from the blanket.

Chanti immediately went for it and Mary sat up quickly and grabbed him even though he wasn't quite going to reach it. He strained to get out of her hands and she could feel the energy pulsing in his body as if electric current were running through it.

Moments later the boy who apparently missed catching the ball ran up to it, bent down, grabbed it with his right hand, and straightened up.

He was a scrawny red-haired kid with a pale freckled face, watery blue eyes, and a badly chipped front tooth, dressed in a collarless white shirt and brown-and-red herringbone tweed wool knickers with a matching hat on his head, its visor turned all the way to the right. His left hand was hidden in a big worn baseball glove that seemed to be half his size.

What is it, a chicken? He asked quizzically as if he had never seen a rooster before.

He's a rooster, Mary replied, holding on to Chanti who was struggling even more strongly to set himself free. He's a boy chicken, she added after a few seconds, trying to clarify the situation, His name is "Alexander" but I call him "Chanti."

Oh, yeah? The boy said, surprised. Roosters have names like people?

He does, Mary replied. He's my son.

Really? The boy said, this time incredulous. You're a hen?

I'm not a hen, Mary said, But I'm a Henley on both my father's and my mother's side, so that's probably why I have him, and added to make herself more believable, His father was part rooster.

Oh, the boy muttered, now thoroughly confused, not knowing what to say, staring at Chanti with big eyes.

112

At that point two other boys from among those who were playing, both without gloves however, came running and stood quietly, watching what was going on. One of them was tall and skinny, with black hair that hung over his forehead like a big right-angle tear in an item of clothing, dressed in a collarless white shirt like the scrawny boy's and black pants with stove-pipe legs that reached to the middle of his calves, supported by a lone suspender running diagonally across his chest. The other one was nondescript, as if hiding behind the other two so that you couldn't see him.

He really wants to see the ball, The scrawny boy said, seeing Chanti struggle. Here, look at it, he continued, squatting down and extending the ball to the former.

Chanti bent forward and lightning-fast pecked at the ball.

Ouch! The boy yelled out in pain, looking at his hand with the ball. A big shiny drop of dark blood stood out on the end of his thumb like a precious jewel. He quickly put the ball in the glove and sucked on his thumb.

While doing that he bent his head forward and once again Chanti with lightning speed struck with his beak at the boy's face, in the vicinity of his right eye near the bridge of the nose. That's where the boy's freckles were most prominent and he must have thought they were grain.

Hey! Jesus, what are you doing?! The boy yelled, shooting straight up and putting his right hand over the spot where he'd been struck. He rubbed it with his fingers for a few seconds and then took them away and looked down. There was no blood at them but a small red spot with the skin slightly broken was visible below the eye in the corner by the bridge of the nose.

I'm sorry! Mary yelled, sitting up and holding on with all her might to Chanti who was struggling more strongly than ever to set himself free, apparently feeling there were good prospects where he'd struck. He must have thought your freckles were grain, she explained.

Your son's a real danger to people, ma'am, the boy yelled, in an angry voice, rubbing the struck spot with his fingers to ease his pain. You ought to keep him locked up in a cage.

Did he hurt me? He asked, concerned, turning to the tall boy and taking his hand away to let the latter see.

The tall boy bent forward, peered closely at the spot, and after a few seconds straighten up and said, No, not much. There's just a red spot there. He barely broke the skin.

You're lucky, you sonofabitch! The scrawny boy yelled at Chanti. I'd have wrung your neck if you'd hurt my eye. Jeepers-Creepers, he continued rubbing his face, slightly calmed down, He'd nearly pecked out my eye....

He turned around and the three boys started to move away.

Wait! Mary shouted. Don't go away. Take him with you. He wants to play with you. He can run fast.

Run fast, The tall boy scoffed. Can he bat, or pitch, or catch?

Yeah, the scrawny boy said, turning around without stopping, Can he do any of that?... But we could put him on second base... tie him up and use him as a cushion. You want to give him to us? And as Mary remained silent, not knowing what to say, he turned

114

around and muttering, The sonofabitch! He nearly pecked out my eye, walked away.

With sadness, almost despair, Mary watched the three grow smaller as they walked.

4. on the staircase

There is a forceful knock on the door and Mary's heart sinks. She's been expecting it for a while and debates whether or not to answer it but after a few seconds decides she will. There's no point avoiding the inevitable. She will have to face it sooner or later, so she might as well do it now.

She walks up to the door and in a weak, shaky voice asks who it is. The chain latch on the door is fastened and she puts her hand on the former to make sure it's in properly, which it is, and waits.

A gruff masculine voice with a heavy Italian accent filters in through the door panel from the outside in response, It's-a me, Mery. Open up-a!

It's her landlord Salvatore Malatesta. He's come to talk about Chanti.

What is it, Mr. Malatesta? Mary asks in a marginally stronger voice, having had time to recover some of her composure. What do you want? I've paid you this month's rent. It's still more than a week before the next one.

Open up-a, Mery! The man responds more gruffly, I didn't come for de rent-a. I want to talk-a to you about de rooster.

What rooster? Mary asks, feigning ignorance. I don't know what you're talking about. There's no rooster here.

Don't-a lie to me, Mery, The man says now in an angry voice. You know you have a rooster in dere. Open de door-a!

Mary feels she has no choice, so she opens the door, leaving the latch on. A fairly wide crack has opened up and through it she sees her landlord's short, stocky figure with a round face and bald head. The chain is strong, but to be safe, she presses her foot against the door down on the floor to make sure the former stays firm.

But Mr. Malatesta, She yells, fully believing her words, I don't have any roosters here.

Yes, you do! The man insists, pushing with his massive body against the door. De oder tenants complain he wakes dem up-a every morning wit his crow.

Oh, Mary replies quickly, following her nimble imagination, It must be because of my dreaming…. I've been having lately these recurring dreams about a rooster crowing. That's what they must have been hearing. I'll make sure I don't dream about him any more.

Hearing a rooster in your dream-a?! The man exclaims, pushing even harder on the door. You craze? What do you tink I em-a— stupid-a? Oder people can't hear your dreams-a. He hits his shoulder against the door, making Mary's foot slip. The chain strains but prevents the door from opening farther however. Open up-a!

Mary presses her foot as strongly as she can against the door and the floor, and yells in despair, I mean I must be crowing in my dream, pretending to be a rooster, so that's what they hear. Like this, she ends, producing a terrible, mushy imitation of a rooster crowing, something like, Khukhurukhuuu!

Dat's supposed to be a rooster crow?! The man yells, his face red with anger. You tink I em an idiot-a! Open up-a!

At that point Chanti who's not been seen or heard so far comes to Mary's rescue, giving out a magnificent, Kikirikiiii! Whereupon Mary immediately steps in, saying, Like this, see?... I was just hoarse. I've cleared my throat.

Dat's a rooster crow alright-a! The man yells, applying more pressure on the door, making the chain strain to the point of breaking. So you have one in dere! You know no pets allowed in de apartment-a. You signed the lease-a. He has to go. Open de door-a!

But he's not a pet, Mr. Malatesta, Mary pleads. He's my son, and I can't let you in. I'm indecent... I mean I'm not dressed. See, she pulls up the hem of her dress as best she can and sticks out her bare leg out for the man to see.

Your son-a?! The man screams, beet-red with anger. You really tink I em an idiot-a! Open up-a! He leans back and throws his shoulder against the door, making the latch come out of the frame, permitting one of his feet to enter the apartment.

At this point something unexpected happens—Chanti appears, his coxcomb swollen blood-red and the feathers around his neck puffed out almost perpendicularly and attacks the man's leg.

117

The latter retreats in terror and Chanti goes after him, attacking various parts of his body, namely the legs, crotch, and behind, not giving up for an instant and jumping progressively higher and higher, making the man scream and eventually turn and run head over heels down the staircase, with Chanti following and attacking him even after the latter stumbles and falls to the floor on the next landing.

Mary runs after them, screaming herself at the top of her voice, Stop, Chanti, stop! All the time painfully aware that she has now no choice how to proceed—the decision has been made for her.

5. in the bar

It's night. Mary is at a nearby bar run by her friend John who has promised to put her up for the night after the place closes. Mary sits on a stool at one end of the bar with Chanti on her lap, facing her friend and nursing a hot toddy he has prepared for her a while back. He's standing up, facing her, having made himself comfortable in the corner, while leaning on the shelves cabinet behind him. At the other end of the bar is the figure of a drunk nearly collapsed on his stool, holding on for dear life to an empty glass on the counter before him. The place is dimly lit, with darkness like vague piles of soft objects stacked up high against the walls, including on top of the tables and chairs that stand there. Among the former, on the floor, there sits a pitiful little heap of Mary's belongings, consisting of two suitcases—one small, the other one large, tied with a twine wrapped twice around it and a large bundle of what looks like bedclothes likewise tied together with the same kind of twine. It's perfectly quiet, no one, including Chanti, making the slightest sound.

The telephone on the wall at the end of the bar where Mary and the bartender are rings, the latter goes over to it, picks up the limp-penis earpiece that hangs down, presses it to his ear, says something short into the mouthpiece, turns around, and speaks loudly to the drunk, It's for you, O'Brien.

The man grumbles something, clearly annoyed, lets go of the helping glass, traces an uneven broken line toward the telephone, takes the earpiece out of the bartender's hand, and says something in an angry voice into the mouthpiece. You can't make out what he says but, from the intonation and the few vowels that are audible, it appears he speaks with a heavy accent.

He remains silent for a while, then says something short in an even angrier voice, breaks the connection by pushing down on the hook with his fingers, and walks away from the phone, leaving the earpiece hanging down, dangling widely from side to side, now no longer resembling a limp penis but a clock pendulum.

Hang up the phone, O'Brien! The bartender shouts angrily at the man, but the latter pays no attention to his words, as if not hearing him, and tries to retrace his previous path to the barstool, missing it pretty much completely however.

Visibly annoyed the bartender walks up to the telephone, hangs up the earpiece, runs after the man who hasn't quite made it back to his stool, puts his hand on the former's shoulder and after saying, You're going home, O'Brien. You've had enough, steers him to the door leading outside. The man offers no resistance to what is being done to him, as if not aware of it, and obediently disappears behind the swinging doors through which he is pushed out which gently sway a few times like the surface of water into which a stone has been dropped.

The bartender goes back to his former place and stands there as before. Not a word has been exchanged between him and Mary as if what had happened had not taken place and none seem to be coming. What has happened is apparently not unusual and is of no interest to either of them.

About minute or two after the bartender has returned to his place a male figure appears in the swinging door. It isn't the drunk however but another man. He's short and slight with a thin, kindly face and thinning black hair and is dressed in a white shirt and gray pants. He walks up to the bar and sits down on the stool next to Mary.

Hi, Frank, the bartender says coming up to the man. How have you been? Haven't seen you for a while.

Been busy at the office, if you know what I mean, the man replies, putting a strange emphasis on the word "office." Almost didn't get to go out tonight. Some customers needed moral support. But I finally calmed them down.... It's good to see you.

What'll you have? The bartender asks. The usual?

No, the man replies, Make it on the rocks... with a little splash of water. Need some hydration after the grief I had to listen to.

OK, the bartender replies before moving away to prepare the man's drink.

The man follows the bartender with his eyes and then turns toward Mary.

What a beautiful rooster! He exclaims, having apparently only then noticed Chanti, whom Mary has been holding pressed tight to her body. What's his name?

Alexander, Mary replies, suddenly animated, woken up from her gloom and stupor by the man's words. But I call him "Chanti," after "Chanticleer," because of his beautiful voice.

He's a beauty, the man says, reaching out with his fingers to stroke Chianti's golden mantel, who shows no sign of recognition of this happening. His eyes are open but it is long past his bedtime.

My name is Frank, the man says, turning to Mary again and offering her his hand. What's yours?

Mary, Mary replies, shaking his. Pleased to meet you.

Mary has finished her drink long time ago. The man notices this and asks if she would have another one, to which she says yes.

Was it a hot toddy? The man asks, guessing from what's left on the bottom of her glass, and when she says yes, again, he says to the bartender, who is just at that instant bringing his drink, And another hot toddy for the lady, John. It's on me.

6. father frank

Mary in the secret bedroom at the rectory, sitting on a red-cushioned bench by the window which is partly shaded by a red velvet curtain, knitting some large pink item of clothing or covering of ill-defined shape. The room cramped, with dark wood paneling and a big four-poster bed with a red canopy over it, covered with an imitation antique-tapestry bedspread, its head against one of the walls. The window narrow, with thin led stiles that form a dense grid, the glass in them thick and slightly flawed but not as much as in old windows. She's been taking her eyes off the knitting from time to time to glance out the window where a dozen or so of chickens—mostly hens, with only a few roosters,

121

Chanti among them—are grazing on the emerald-green lawn in the courtyard between the church and the rectory open on one end. The church and the structure that joins the former to the rectory built in neogothic style of neatly cut light gray stone.

The door opens and Frank—father Frank—wearing the black suit, shirt, and stiff white collar of a priest comes in, closing the door behind him.

You're still knitting the thing? He says, coming up to Mary and looking at what she has produced. It's going to be a big baby—a stork or an eagle this time.

I haven't unraveled it for a while, Mary replies without taking her eyes off the knitting, so it has grown. I'll do it soon.

Did you notice how they all gather around him as if around a teacher? She says finally lifting her eyes and gazing out the window. … Like the disciples and those who came to hear Christ preach around him, she concludes.

Father Frank comes up to the window and looks outside.

You're right, he says after a while, They're all nipping at the grass but it's as if they're following him, doing what he's doing and getting something out of it.

Yeah, Mary says, having stopped to knit. I've been thinking that since chickens don't talk, doing things like pecking or nipping grass is for them like speaking is for us.

Yes, father Frank says. It's possible.

So, maybe Chanti is chickens' Christ and God has sent him down to save them the way he sent down Christ to save people. After all, my name's "Mary."

You know, you may be right, Father Frank says in an earnest voice after a moment's hesitation. I've noticed how different he is from other chickens and how they all congregate around him, and then how he was born, and now that your name's "Mary".... It's possible. God's ways are mysterious.

It'd always bothered me, He continues after a moment of silence, That we believe that only people have souls and that God cares only about us. But maybe it's not true. Maybe all creatures have souls—different souls than ours, smaller, animal souls—and God cares about them too. So maybe that's why Chanti came into the world—to save chickens. So, there're probably Christs for other animals—cows, horses, cats, dogs, and so on... and even amebae. After all, God, sent other messengers to people whom Christ couldn't reach, like Mahomed and Buddha. So maybe that's what Chanti is.

My God! Mary exclaims, raising her eyes skyward, an expression of meekness and bliss on her face like those on Virgin Mary's in old paintings. That's what it must be.

I just hope they don't crucify him this time, she adds in a whisper.

7. holy ghost

It was a recurring dream, it was reality, it was a disaster.

It was Easter Sunday and Mary ensconced herself with Chanti behind the altar, pressed against its cold marble, huddling on a low stool and clutching Chanti to her bosom, listening to the

123

solemn mass being conducted on the other side by father Frank, and when, after blessing the host and putting it on top of the folded white cloth draped over the chalice he placed the latter on the altar, turned his back to it, and facing the church audience with his arms raised high and wide, called out in his strong clear voice the appropriate words in Latin, Chanti, whose body had all along been vibrating with pent-up energy as if with electric current, apparently prodded by what he heard, flew out of Mary's arms, landed on the altar, and likewise spreading his wings wide and high as if in imitation of father Frank, looking like a dark and angry holy ghost, let out a loud and crystal-clear "Kikirikiiii" that drowned out father Franks words, releasing at the same time from the audience a huge wave of laughter mixed with screams of surprise and fear. He then jumped at the chalice and with one powerful peck split the host in two, tipping the chalice forward and letting the red wine in it spill over the immaculate white cloth with which the altar was covered.

8. farmer floyd

The following was said in a loud stern voice accompanied by a long finger pointing in rhythm with the words by farmer Floyd, dressed in a red plaid lumberjack shirt and faded denim overalls, looking like a tall biblical patriarch or prophet with long luxurious gray hair but sans moustache and beard, in the living room of his family farmhouse with its walls covered by wallpaper of huge red roses or peonies on a shocking pink background, decorated in the cloying Victorian style with elaborately carved dark wood furniture and all sort of bric-a-brac by his late wife Mabel: I love you dearly, Mary, but this has got to stop! My gold watch—broken, the grandfather clock—broken (I still don't know how he got up there), the fuel gage in the new Studebaker—broken, the lock to the safe—unusable, my favorite cow Molly's eye pecked out, all those sacks pecked through and the barn half-filed with wheat….

It was because you locked him up there for punishment, Mary said pleadingly. He's a man, Floyd, I mean a male, and he's young. Remember what you told me you used to do when you were young? You were no different. But look at how the hens are laying eggs now, how happy they are.

The hens, is fine, farmer Floyd replied, I don't deny that. But this constant destruction has got to stop! I'm telling you, Mary, if it doesn't, and especially if one more time, one single time he goes after my eye, he's roadkill, Mary, I'm telling you, he's roadkill!

9. roadkill

It was a recurring dream, it was reality, it was a disaster, it was the end.

Mary had advance notice since farmer Floyd ran first for the hoe, so she had a good two hundred feet lead on him as she was running as fast as she could in her short woman's stride made shorter by her skirt and slippers on her feet down the country road, clutching Chanti with all her might to her chest, but he was gaining on her, covering the ground in his enormous tall man's strides, his biblical hair flying, his face twisted in a scary grimace from hate and exertion, his eyes ablaze even when seen from that distance, the long hoe in his hand like a giant conducting baton interpreting the most overdramatic, overemotional, over the top musical composition, but when he was some hundred feet behind her there was the roar of a car engine and the front of a big expensive car barreling down the road toward her appeared from behind the bend—a shiny grinning-through-teeth grill, two giant googling chrome-plated headlights spaced far apart and another two smaller normal ones spaced closer together below, all framed on both sides by a pair of maroon fenders.

125

Mary slowed down a little trying to keep her eyes on the car as she ran looking over her shoulder, but when it was about to pass her felt something hard and sharp hit her left eye and at the same time Chanti free himself from her arms and fly toward the middle of the road.

There was incredible pain all over her face and head, the sound of a car horn blowing desperately and of car breaks screeching wildly while being applied full-force, followed by an explosion of black feathers shooting up into the air like oil gushing up from the ground as the car was passing her by.

But then it slowed down and came to a stop, spun to the left, its long maroon, cream, and chrome body blocking the road, its front wheels with their white-walled tires in the ditch, about a hundred feet away.

10. millionaire mike
(chanti, my son!)

Mary rolled over on her back. For a few seconds the ceiling was just an expanse of gray stretching down toward her feet and to the sides but then awareness of her surroundings began to creep into her mind and she remembered where she was.

They'd landed in Le Havre the previous morning and after disembarking, what with going through the customs, especially with the car and all, didn't get on the road before late afternoon, and having gotten lost in the countryside while driving to Rouen where they were to attend a conference with a bunch of oil executives, her husband Mike's colleagues, and it getting dark, decided to spend the night at a roadside farm which had the sign "*Chambres*" hung out on a post.

The wax with which she'd plugged up her ears as always bothered her, so she took it out and put it down on the bedside table next to the maroon eye patch, her watch, and items of jewelry she'd left there before going to bed.

Mike was a champion snorer and she had to use earplugs when they slept together, but although this time he was sleeping in the next room, because the bed there stood with its headboard against the adjacent wall, which was thin, his snoring was keeping her awake, so she had to use them after all.

He apparently was still asleep but was no longer snoring, as happened sometimes. It was still all around.

She felt good. They had dined on buckwheat crepes with grilled sausages washed down with homemade hard cider, followed by a *gâteau normand* topped with whipped cream and a calvados served in a warmed-up snifter for a nightcap, and the thought of what she might have for breakfast filled her with energy. She would get up.

She threw back the covers, jumped out of bed, ran up to the window, threw it wide open, and filled her lungs with air. The room was on the second floor and the world spread out wide before her.

It was a glorious May morning. The sky was clear, the air fresh and filled with the happy chirping of birds. Their car, the Duesenberg maroon and cream model SJ sweep panel phaeton, its top up, stood next to the fence about a hundred feet away, its dew-drenched body, especially the chrome-plated parts, sparkling like a diamond in the sunlight.

The house and the farm buildings, all in the timbered Normandy style, formed a large court with one side—the one along the road—

127

open. There were a few carts and some farm machinery, including a small tractor, scattered around haphazardly all over it and a large mound of earth for some reason stood in its middle. A bunch of chickens were busy digging in it, apparently looking for worms, and suddenly there was heard the crowing of a rooster. He was scrawny and nondescript but had climbed to the top of the mound and was proclaiming his reign over the yard from there.

His call was feeble and hoarse, nothing like the strong and clear one of Chanti, but it brought the latter's presence and absence to Mary's mind, and it was as if a powerful blow had been delivered to her head—her face crumbled like the proverbial cookie, breaking up into parts which, it seemed, could never be put together again.

Doing the utmost to force her broken mouth info forming words, her eyes—the good right one and the ugly white blind left one—filling with tears, she whispered barely audibly, Chanti, my son!

clara not schumann but fick

a mininovel

1. not brahms

The dining/living room of Clara's apartment. Big and square. White walls have turned gray probably more due to the quality of paint than age. Also dirty. No pictures on them. Instead, their surfaces like big abstract canvases depicting an absence of forms. A long rectangular table with a white Formica top and thin (too thin) chrome (steel?) legs in the middle. Matching chrome (steel?) chairs (the frame made from the same size tubing and therefore not seeming thin) with Formica seats and backs around it, some badly chipped. The chairs, three on each of the longer sides of the table and one on each of the shorter ones. Something reminiscent of a hospital about the table and chairs, especially the former. A lamp with a big round white enameled shade hanging down low from the ceiling over the table. The shade pristine, not chipped anywhere. In the corner of one of the walls parallel to the longer sides of the table a rectangular opening leading to a hallway. The hallway dark. To the left of the opening a long sofa about two thirds of the width of the wall with a chrome (definitely chrome) frame and blood-red imitation suede cushions. The cushions worn, almost black in places. In the middle of the wall on the left a big window, also about two thirds of the width of the wall. The world beyond it invisible in thick fog. (It is fall, early morning.) Soft milky light streaming into the room as a result. On the windowsill a can of sardines, unopened. No two red cherries joined at the end of their stems next to it. In the corner on the left of the window directly on the floor a largish metal (tin?) toy piano (prepared?). A piano is *de rigueur* in a place inhabited by a Schumann even if a "Not" one. In the opposite corner along the wall a narrow white

131

door, crooked like a man with one shoulder lower than the other. The door shut. In the middle of the next wall on the left a big white French door with rippled red glass panels. The glass sealed with white paper on the other side. This door also shut. On the left of the door in the corner of the wall with the sofa along it the opening to the hallway.

Faint shuffling is heard coming from the hallway like that made by mice rummaging. Two figures emerge from it—a woman and a man. It is Clara Not Schumann and Not Brahms. She has brought him to show him her apartment. They are walking on tiptoes, Not Brahms following Clara. He moves reluctantly as if being pulled by his arm or a blind man led by someone he doesn't quite trust. On coming into the room Not Brahms stops. When Clara notices this she does the same. She is dressed in a white nurse's outfit—dress, stockings, shoes. No white cap with a red cross in the middle of it on her head. Not Brahms wears a gray tweed suit made out of a thick material. His left hand is heavily bandaged. He holds it up and presses it to his chest like something very dear to him, for instance his newborn child.

Clara *(peeved, speaking in a whisper; the conversation continues in a whisper from then on until noted otherwise):* Come on, come on!

Not Brahms *(visibly uncomfortable, doesn't budge):* But what if he's in? *("He" is her husband Not Schumann.)*

Clara *(peeved again, dismissive):* It doesn't matter. If he's in we'll tell him you've come to look at the apartment... to buy it.

Not Brahms *(shocked, his eyes grown round):* But I'm not. I'm not interested in buying it. I can't.

132

Clara *(same as before, perhaps even more so):* It's just an alibi. Don't worry. He's probably asleep anyway if he's in. He's always asleep. Come on!

She moves forward and proceeds counterclockwise in the order specified above around the room like a guide in a museum trying to expose Not Brahms to all of its attractions. He follows still hesitant but outwardly pacified. (Inside his misgivings persist.) Stays away from the sofa as if afraid it might hurt him. (Afraid of the sharp edges of its metal frame? the color of the cushions? their nature? them being worn?) Looks around with interest around the room however. Devotes a lot of time to walls. Seems to see the invisible canvases mentioned above on them. Likes them. The floor creaks peevishly under their feet (toes). The creaking faint however so that it doesn't worry Not Brahms. As far as Clara is concerned it doesn't exist—much louder sounds wouldn't worry her.

The two move past the window. Not Brahms is puzzled by the can of sardines. Would like to ask why it is there but doesn't. It would be tactless. (He is of the very tactful type.) Subconsciously notices the absence of the two cherries. Misses them. He and Clara come to the corner with the piano. He notices it. Is puzzled by it. Clara notices this and reacts.

Clara *(enthusiastically):* It has a wonderful sound.

She squats down in front of the piano so as to demonstrate the sound it makes to Not Brahms. Her knees are spread wide and feet splayed which reminds Not Brahms of something but he doesn't know what. The only thing he is sure of is that it is something negative. He tries to resolve this question for a few seconds but then gives up. He has to devote his attention to what is happening. Clara's fingers are about to strike the keys but she stops herself at the last moment for obvious reason. Not Brahms understands why and is relieved she has made this decision. Feels as if he has been saved from a disaster.

Clara doesn't explain herself but merely stands up and moves along to the next corner and faces the crooked door. Not Brahms follows her. She opens the door and steps inside. Makes room for Not Brahms to come in. He steps inside.

The room is small, dark (the single window hidden behind a tall piece of furniture—a wardrobe? high-boy?—pushed flush against it, only smudges of light coming out from behind it like chalk dust clinging to the wall), crammed with stuff like a storage room. The shapes of the objects merge, at times making it hard to tell what they are. (Is that a bed in the corner or a long chest with a blanket over it?) Candles stuck on many (most) of the horizontal surfaces. Many of the candles nearly gone, the remaining shapes deformed, sad. Melted wax in big frozen murky pools around them.

Clara *(proudly):* This is my room. Here I'm myself. *(Not Brahms' attention is drawn to the candles. He is puzzled by them. Clara notices this, explains.)* Candles are my passion. They bring light into my life.

Not Brahms understands her but his puzzlement persists. Passion is alright but that many candles? She doesn't notice his puzzlement persists however.

There is a big colored photograph of a red spindly-legged colt on a wall over a cluttered desk. The colt unsteady on its legs, as if on ice, looking quizzically into the camera. It attracts Not Brahms' attention. Clara notices this one.

134

Clara *(quickly, as if grabbing something out of his hand which he shouldn't have):* That was our son's colt.

Clearly averse to the topic she turns around brusquely and walks out of the room.

Not Brahms follows her and she shuts the door after him. He is puzzled again, this time more than before. Thinks. Why doesn't she want to say more about the colt? "Was" means they no longer have it. It couldn't be so because it was sold or given away against her wishes however. She doesn't appear to be the kind of woman who agrees to something she doesn't want and besides it wouldn't be in keeping with her apparent standing *vis-à-vis* her husband. She is clearly the one who wears pants in the family. But if she got rid of the colt of her own volition she most likely wouldn't have its picture on the wall because the colt wouldn't have meant that much to her. It must have died then. That would explain it. She must have been very fond of it and doesn't want to dwell on the subject. Letting a picture hang on the wall is different—it is keeping the memory alive. And her son? There is no sign of him anywhere in the apartment and she hasn't mentioned him before. It couldn't be that he has moved out. She is too young to have a grown-up son. What is she, thirty-five, thirty-seven? He could be a teenager at the most. Maybe he is in a boarding school? Although that is unlikely since nobody sends their kids to boarding school these days. At least he hasn't heard of anyone. Are there any boarding schools left? He hasn't heard of any.

The French door with the red glass panels is on their right. Clara walks up to it, bends down, and looks in through the keyhole. She stays in this position for a long time. Not Brahms sees what is happening and his musings about the colt and Clara's son are pushed out by his wondering what Clara is doing. Why is she peering in and for such a long time? Is there something wrong inside? Is something going on with her husband?

Not Brahms *(in a loud whisper):* What's happening? *(After no answer comes back from Clara.)* Is something wrong?

Clara straightens up and comes back to Not Brahms.

Clara *(whispering in his ear):* He's in there... asleep. *(Takes his arm and pulls him toward the door.)* Look! *(Not Brahms resists her. The very idea of his spying on her husband through the keyhole is horrifying to him.)* Go on. *(She keeps insisting as he resists her.)* Go!

Terrified though that he is, Not Brahms lets himself be pulled by Clara's hand toward the door but pretends he is refusing to obey her and will prevail in the end. This clearly will not happen. Eventually he stands by the door, feels his head being pushed down by Clara, and obediently gives in to her. He realizes his injured hand is pressed to his chest where his heart is, presses it stronger with his other hand, bends all the way down, and looks through the keyhole.

At first he isn't aware of what he sees—just an expanse of white—but then realizes that straight in front of him, in the middle of the room, no more than three feet away from the door, stands a bed with a person stretched out on it under a white sheet. The bed is high as those in a hospital but unusually long so that its head and foot aren't visible. The person's head and feet aren't visible either and Not Brahms realizes with amazement the former must be extremely tall, more than two meters (six foot seven)... two meters five, ten, fifteen (seven feet plus) or even taller.

He realizes then it must be Clara's husband Not Schumann and is seized by an uncontrollable fear as if the man might harm him. The man's height seems to play an important part in this. He straightens up instantly and turns toward Clara.

Not Brahms *(with shivers running up his spine):* He's very tall. Two meters ten... fifteen....

Clara *(dismissively):* Two meters three (six foot eight). *(Drops the topic but clearly not for the same reason as that of the colt. She doesn't deem it interesting.)* Would you like some coffee?

Not Brahms drinks tea but is glad to have a way of getting away from the door. He will take care of the details later.

Not Brahms: Yes.

Clara heads for the opening to the hallway and he follows her. They enter the hallway. Inside, it doesn't seem as dark as appears from the room. Not Brahms sees the outline of a door on his left. Clara notices this, stops, and opens the door half-way. It is totally dark inside. She flips a switch but no light comes on.

Clara: The light's burnt out. I have to put in a new bulb.

Not Brahms is puzzled once more. Isn't there a widow there? The wall faces outside.

Not Brahms *(can't resist giving in to his puzzlement):* Isn't there a window there?

Clara: We have walled it up. It's more intimate that way.

She shuts the door. Moves along. Not Brahms follows with a residue of puzzlement in him. Intimacy is alright but a window is a plus in a bathroom. Decides not to dwell on his puzzlement however. They move on, come to another door. Clara opens it and steps inside. Not Brahms follows her.

He is in shock. The room is obviously a kitchen but looks like a dungeon. The walls and ceiling are not painted white and smooth as in the rest of the apartment but gray and coarse as if made from concrete. The ceiling is vaulted and seems higher than in the rest of the apartment again. There is only one window in the room, square and small, high up under the ceiling in the far right corner. Under the window, its head in the corner and one side along the wall on the right, stands a narrow bed, what looks like three-quarter size, with a rusty iron frame, a thin mattress covered with a gray blanket, and a dirty striped white and blue flat pillow without a cover. Smack in the middle of the wall facing the door stands a small old white refrigerator with a convex door. It is dwarfed by the size and emptiness of the wall. Against the wall on the left, starting with the far corner, are an old-fashioned white enameled sink, attached to it, next a similarly old-fashioned and white gas stove with four burners, and finally white metal cabinets with a white Formica top which extend all the way to the wall with the door in it. In the middle of the room stands a square table with a white Formica top and tubular steel legs similar to the one in the dining/living room and four matching chairs with white Formica seats and backs and tubular legs, one at each of the sides. The Formica on the counter top, table, and chairs badly chipped in places. A lamp with a big round white enameled shade identical to the one in the dining/living room hanging down high from the ceiling. The shade chipped in a few places, one of them badly. The floor in the room is definitely concrete.

Not Brahms is stunned. He doesn't know what to think. How can the ceiling in the kitchen be higher than in the rest of the apartment? Is it only an illusion? The kitchen has clearly been remodeled but why this way? To make it look old-fashioned? Old-fashioned is understandable but why like a dungeon? Was the original window walled up and the small one put in at the same time that the bathroom window was walled up? Is the bed their son's? Is this where he sleeps/slept? But why was he banished to this dungeon of a kitchen?

Clara on the other hand is energized. Apparently no longer feeling she has to restrain herself so as not to be heard by her husband she walks up in a normal stride to the stove and turns toward Not Brahms. A sign of displeasure appears on her face.

Clara *(loudly, in a testy voice):* Shut the door and come on over here!

2. *träumerei* 1
(the colt)

Clara is in her living room. Their son's colt is running around in it and her husband is trying to catch it. Clara is standing on the sofa and screams at him to be quick about it. The colt is knocking things over and he might break something. Her husband is clumsy and the colt keeps getting away. His being in his bathrobe doesn't make things easier for him. Clara screams for her husband to take his bathrobe off but he doesn't heed her. She is boiling mad. He never does anything right! The colt knocks over a chair, then another one, she is sure they are getting chipped, then the colt hits with its hoof the toy piano in the corner and the poor thing gives out a wild terrified sound. The colt rounds the table and jumps up onto the sofa nearly pushing her off it. She fights back and gives the colt a shove. It goes flying down on the floor and lands on it like a big splash of flesh. It remains lying on its left side keeping its right front leg up. It appears the leg might be badly injured, perhaps broken. Clara is worried about the colt, jumps off the sofa, and bends over the animal. It lies still holding its leg up. It must be broken for sure! Clara slaps the colt on the neck hoping against hope to rouse it, it raises its head, looks at her plaintively, but stays lying down. Its sad eyes say it can't get up because its leg hurts.

Clara knows what it means for a horse to have its leg broken. It is essentially finished. It is very hard to heal such a thing. Horses are usually put away when this happens.

She remembers her husband has a gun. She turns to him and tells him to get it. He looks her in the eye indicting he knows what she has in mind and that he agrees with her. He goes into his room, comes back with the gun, and hands it to her. It is a revolver with a big cylinder and a long barrel.

She takes it and turns to the colt. It raises is head and looks at her plaintively as it had done before. Its huge round eye is perfectly black and unbelievably sad. Clara aims the gun at the colt's head, pulls the trigger, and fires. A dry sound is heard and a cloud of white smoke hides the colt's head from her. When it dissipates the colt's head lies on the floor, its eye still open but now looking merely dead instead of sad. The hole where the bullet entered is above the eye. It is round and also black but tiny and no blood comes out of it.

Clara mechanically turns around and faces her husband. He stands a few feet away, his face pale and expressionless. Mechanically, without consciously deciding to do this Clara raises the gun, aims it at his forehead, pulls the trigger, and fires. Once again a dry sound is heard and a cloud of white smoke hides her husband's face. She can feel a thumping sound on the floor and something soft touch her feet as this happens. When the smoke dissipates her husband is no longer standing before her. With the lower part of her peripheral vision she sees he lies in a heap at her feet.

She doesn't look at his body but drops the gun on top of it so that it makes no noise and turns toward the table. There is a bowl of cherries sitting in the middle of it. Clara steps over the body, gets the bowl, and goes up to the window. It is open and she stands in the middle of it. She remains standing there looking outside eating cherries and spitting the pits out into the yard.

There are boys playing in it down below, about four or five of them. They run around chasing each other, making blood-curdling screams, except for one who is sitting on a tricycle looking down at the handlebar and doing something on it with his hands. He seems to be trying to fix something. He is right below the window next to the tree that grows there. Clara has just finished eating a cherry and she takes the pit in her fingers and throws it at him, hitting him in the middle of the head.

The boy puts his hand on the spot where he was hit, raises his head, and looks around nervously. He searches the yard with his eyes and doesn't seem to consider the possibility of having been hit from a floor above.

Clara smiles inwardly and livens up. She steps back from the window so that it would be harder for the boy to see her, puts a cherry in her mouth, eats it, takes the pit in her hand, and throws it at the boy.

He has given up searching around by now, has gone back to trying to fix the handlebar, and is looking down at it. The pit hits him smack in the middle of the head again.

141

This time he doesn't touch his head but jerks it up even more quickly and looks around in anger.

It seems this time he might eventually look up, and Clara quickly jumps over to the left side of the window, hides behind the wall, and presses against it. This time she laughs openly with a short, breathy laughter, puts a fresh cherry in her mouth, and eats it. She takes the pit out and holds it in her hand. She will wait a few seconds before looking out to see if the boy has gone back to fixing his tricycle, and if he has she will move out and throw the pit at him.

3. sardines

The living room of Clara's apartment, early in the morning once again. The apartment dead still. Everything as before except the windowsill is empty and the keyhole of the French door is stuffed up with white paper from the other side. A sharp edge of it sticks out so that it would hurt the eye of anyone trying to look in. It would probably even hurt the ear of anyone trying to listen in.

Clara and Not Brahms alone next to the window. The world outside it enveloped in a thick fog as the last time but the light coming in is not milky except of an unhealthy pallor like the complexion of a person suffering from leukemia. Clara and Not Brahms dressed as the last time, he without the bandage on his hand however. No sign of injury on his hand. Particles of moisture glistening on their hair, faces, and clothes like silver dust. They have just come in. Not Brahms hasn't noticed the absence of the two imaginary red cherries from the last time but subconsciously misses the white cap with the red cross on Clara's head he hadn't missed before. This might have something to do with the light bringing to mind leukemia.

142

Clara *(unexpectedly turning to Not Brahms and boring through him with her eyes; in a normal voice):* Why don't you buy the apartment?

Not Brahms *(startled, a vast abyss opening up inside him he never suspected was there):* Me? Buy? *(His blood pounds in his ears so that he has trouble hearing himself talk. Composes himself somewhat.)* I don't know.... *(Swallows hard.)* I don't need an apartment.... I mean I haven't thought of buying one.

Clara *(insistent, still boring through Not Brahms with her eyes):* It's a good deal... a great location. You wouldn't have trouble renting it. In fact we'll rent it back from you. You'll get your money back in a few years.... And you'll have the apartment for nothing.

Not Brahms *(blushing, feeling hot all over):* But... but I don't need an apartment. I've never been a landlord. I hate to take care of things... worry.

Clara *(no change):* We'll take care of everything... just as now. You'll just own the place. There'll be no other difference.

Not Brahms feels Clara is right. Is terrified by the discovery. Chills run up his spine. He will have to go through with the deal... clean out his savings accounts... sell all his assets... go through the bothersome legal channels.... What a hassle! He wishes he wouldn't be there... would miraculously disappear and appear in another place... whisked up and deposited by a time machine.

In the meantime time has passed and he hasn't said anything.

Clara *(thinking he is resisting, being generous):* Why don't you think about it?

143

Not Brahms remains silent, still in a state of shock.

Clara *(surprised Not Brahms has more of a backbone than she thought; but a glimmer of hope remains):* OK?

Not Brahms *(glad to hear the word, relieved as if having emptied his bladder which was about to burst):* OK.

Clara *(also relieved, wants to change the subject so as not to lose what she has gained):* You hungry?

Not Brahms *(surprised again, but in a different way—doesn't know where this comes from):* Nnnooo....

Clara pays no attention to what Not Brahms has said. She knows better than him how he feels. She walks out of the room and Not Brahms hears her walk down the hallway into the kitchen and then sounds of her puttering around there. He has turned partly toward the hallway and waits with apprehension for what is in store for him. Soon he hears Clara's determined footsteps coming down the hallway toward him and she appears carrying an open sardine can and a fork. She walks up to the window and faces him.

Clara *(in a friendly voice):* Do you like sardines?

Not Brahms doesn't know how he will answer but gets no chance to find out. Clara scoops up a piece of a sardine and thrusts it at his lips. He leans back, keeping his mouth closed, finding the idea of the food revolting, but the fork with the sticky substance touches his lips and he opens them instinctively, takes what he is being offered in his mouth, and starts chewing on it. It is mushy and sticky with oil, insipid except for the bits of skin which taste like iron flakes. The bones are crunchy like dirt and the tail on the end seems human eyelashes stuck together, still attached to the

144

eyelid. Unable to stand it he swallows the food and is not sure this has helped.

Clara scoops up a bigger piece and puts it in her mouth.

Clara *(while chewing, her words coated with oil):* I love sardines.... Live on them.... They're very good for you.... Have lots of calcium which women need.... Especially the older ones. But it's good for those that will soon get old too... as a preventative... to store up the calcium.... And even for those that still have a way to go before they get old.... Like me. *(Laughs a nervous laughter. Scoops up more sardine and puts it in her mouth as if to fuel her speech.)* I saw a movie once. Don't remember what it's called.... German.... Where a woman kills herself eating sardines.... She loves them so much. *(Changes the tone of her voice.)* She has a little boy... a drummer.... He's a genius.... Drums all the time.... Destroys one drum after another... Even the tin ones.

Curiosity has started to replace the revulsion inside Not Brahms. He wonders if Clara is talking about Volker Schlöndorff's *The Tin Drum* based on Günter Grass' novel, having gotten it all screwed up.

4. *träumerei* 2
(the hussar)

This seems to take place in some exotic southern country—Spain or France. Clara is walking down narrow stone steps as if into a wine cellar behind a man dressed in military garb—a hussar. His tunic is black with silver piping and there is some red on his epaulettes and collar. The man is very tall with black curly hair and she feels handsome in a coarse masculine way. She doesn't see his face right now but that is what she seems to remember

145

the man looks like. They have just met in the street above and he has invited her to have a drink with him at the place.

They come to the landing at the foot of the stairs, the man opens the door, and they step inside. It is a huge brightly lit room with shiny parquet floor empty of people with only a big black grand piano and a bench at the keyboard in the middle of it. This doesn't surprise her as if she had forgotten about her expectation and is open to any scenario.

They walk toward the piano as if to perform at it—she playing and he singing. She is sure he has a powerful deep voice and will sing beautifully. She is looking forward to it.

The man is as she has remembered/expected him to look, with a strong masculine fleshy face and a luxuriant black mustache rakishly turned up at the ends. He stops at the piano and smiles as she comes up to him and puts his arms around her—his left one around her shoulders and right one around her waist, pressing her pelvis to himself. Because of his height her pelvis presses against his thighs. Something hard and hot under his clothes presses against her midriff—his erect penis.

She gets excited. She forgets about the prospect of them performing at the piano and throws her head back for him to kiss her. He bends down and kisses her on the lips. She feels his mustache tickle her face and tastes his fleshy juicy mouth.

The kiss goes on for a while, she has to catch her breath, and tears her mouth away from his with a laugh. He also laughs and is out of breath and they disengage themselves from each other.

There is a bulge under his tunic on the left side where his heart is and, intrigued, she touches the spot wanting to solve the mystery.

The hussar makes a serious face, sticks his hand inside his tunic, and pulls out something white and fluffy—a rabbit! They both explode with laughter—he is like a magician who has pulled a rabbit out of a hat.

The hussar shows her the rabbit. It is adorable—fluffy and snow-white with pink eyes and nose. She wants to take it in her hands but the hussar moves away and then suddenly lunges forward and shoves the rabbit under her skirt, between her legs.

She screams with surprise and joy, jumps away, but remains standing there looking at him and laughing. The hussar laughs too and prepares to lunge forward once more and stick the rabbit under her skirt as before. He does lunge, she evades him, runs around the piano, and he follows her.

They make a few turns around the piano and in the end he manages to catch her and squeezes the rabbit between her legs. She feels its soft warm body between her thighs and melts with submission.

Then the rabbit is gone and she and the hussar are on top of the piano, she face up on her back, he face down on top of her, her feet on the piano, legs bent in the knees and spread, his body between them. He is making love to her, pounding with his pelvis against the back of her thighs rhythmically like a machine. She closes her eyes abandoning herself to him, waiting for the pleasure to come.

It doesn't come however. All she feels is that they are sliding down the top of the piano toward the edge. Soon her head is over the edge and is about to hang down.

She stops him from moving and pushes both of them toward the middle of the piano. He does his part moving back too and once there the pounding resumes.

She lets this go on, once again expecting the pleasure to come, but it still doesn't, and they once more reach the edge of the piano and move back as before.

The third time around she gets angry—why doesn't he do something about them sliding? She expects him to have spurs on his boots (she hasn't seen them earlier but is sure he has them on) and he could dig them into the piano and thus stop them from sliding. (She doesn't think how he could do it with them being on his heels and sticking up into the air.)

She tells him to do this but he doesn't seem to hear her and goes on pounding away against her like a machine. Then she realizes why she doesn't feel any pleasure. He is fully dressed, with his penis inside his pants, and so is she, with her panties on. He has failed to unbutton his fly and to undress her. He seems not to know how to make love, the idiot! Perhaps he is still a virgin.

At this point she realizes they have reached the edge of the piano again, farther moreover than on the two occasions before. Her head is hanging way down, the hussar makes one more shove with his pelvis, and they go flying off the piano onto the floor.

It is as if the ceiling in the room had come down. Everything seems topsy-turvy and when she gets herself together they are lying side by side on the floor.

She is very angry with him and starts pounding away at him with her fists.

He doesn't defend himself but lies rolled up in the fetal position, his fists protecting his face.

She looks at him closer and sees he is not a hussar at all but a boy ten to twelve years old dressed in his black school uniform with silver piping.

5. *träumerei* 3
(cherries)

Not Brahms is standing by the window in Clara's living room, looking out. It is open and in the tree that grows in front of it sits Clara eating cherries. She is wearing a dress and is holding them in her lap. The tree must be a cherry tree and she must have picked them off it but he doesn't see any berries among the leaves. Either Clara has picked them all off or he merely doesn't see them. He isn't concentrating on them so it is the latter that is likely. He watches Clara with great interest.

She puts a cherry in her mouth and eats it, looking at him. The expression on her face is friendly. She seems to be trying to smile at him. She finishes eating, spits the pit out, and asks with a gesture and expression on her face if he would like to have one. He nods that he would.

Clara takes a cherry and throws it to him. He tries to catch it with his hand but misses it and it falls to the ground. He looks plaintively at Clara.

She is already eating another cherry but takes one more from her lap and throws it to him. She has aimed well but he clumsily misses it again and it once more falls to the ground.

Clara shrugs her shoulders indicating that there is nothing she can do. She spits the pit out and gestures for him to join her in the tree. He finds the prospect of jumping over too daunting and doesn't react to her suggestion. She keeps urging him on to do it however and in the end he begins to react. At first he indicates with gestures that he can't do it and then that he isn't sure if he can. She keeps urging him on and on however and in the end he finds himself standing on the windowsill facing the tree. The window is too short for him and he has to bend down to stand up in it.

The ground is far below however and he is terrified and is holding onto the window frame with his left hand. He doesn't think he will be able to reach it. Clara urges him now with words telling him not to be a coward and jump. She says it isn't very far and since she has done it he too will be able to do it. She repeats for him not to be a coward.

He can't stand the taunting and in spite of not being sure if he can reach the tree he jumps. As soon as he does this he realizes he hasn't put enough force into the jump. He will not reach the tree. Nonetheless he stretches out his arms as he nears Clara but he is too far away from and below her and even though she reaches out to him he can't grab her hands and keeps on falling. He looks down and sees there is a child's tricycle standing at the foot of the tree and he is falling directly on it. He grows numb imagining what it will do to him.

6. *träumerei* 4
(bitch)

Not Brahms and Clara are walking down a busy city street with a lot of traffic in it and people on the sidewalks. They have just gotten off the train and have come to the city to visit the grave of

Clara's little boy who died years ago. They walk side by side but Clara leads the way. She knows the city and he has never been to it.

Suddenly Clara speeds up so that she gets ahead of him. He speeds up right away too so that in a few seconds he is again alongside her and they walk together. There is an intersection of two streets about a hundred feet up ahead. It must have something to do with the grave. The cemetery must be nearby there.

Actually it is not an intersection of two streets but a smaller street branching off from or feeding into a bigger one. The bigger street is the continuation of the street he and Clara are on. The smaller street branches off from/feeds into it on the left. The angle between the two streets is very sharp. There is a small triangular open space between the two streets with a few trees and benches under them in it. It is a park of sorts except a very small one and it seems abandoned. The trees look stunted and the ground under them is bare, covered with dirt and pebbles, with garbage scattered here and there over it. There is also a stone fountain on a pedestal in the middle of the space with the figure in the center of it damaged so that it is hard to tell what it is. It is a human figure however for sure. There is no water running in the fountain. Its bowl looks dry. It must be late fall for there are few leaves on the trees—some still green but mostly yellow.

Clara is walking faster and faster as if trying to catch a bus about to depart and he has a hard time keeping up with her. He is afraid ultimately he won't be able to do it. They have almost reached the point where the two streets meet/branch and are along the middle of the little park on their left. As was said the traffic in the street is heavy but suddenly a gap opens up in it and Clara dashes across the street to the other side. He wants to follow her but there is a

151

car coming from the opposite direction and he knows he won't be able to make it. Reluctantly he stops and watches with disappointment Clara get up onto the sidewalk on the other side and continue on into the park. He wants to be with her but there is too much traffic for him to cross the street. He waits but cars keep on coming in both directions. He sees Clara stroll in the park looking at the ground as if searching for something. He is concerned he is not with her. He feels again his place is at her side.

Suddenly a small gap in the traffic opens up again. It is smaller than the previous one but he decides to take a chance and dashes across the street. The oncoming car on the other side doesn't slow down and he almost gets run over by it. He feels the wind made by it on his clothes. He is wearing a loose coat and its long skirt blows in the draft.

When he comes into the park Clara is still walking around looking down on the ground searching for something. He comes up to her and asks what she is doing. She doesn't answer him but he doesn't press her. He is afraid to get her angry. He knows how short-tempered she is. Besides he knows what she is looking for anyway—her son's grave.

He is sure of this now but still is puzzled. Why would a body be buried in a city park? He wonders for a while and in the end explains to himself the place must have been a cemetery once which was converted into a park. Perhaps the city has grown. Abandoned cemeteries are frequently taken over for other uses. He knows Clara hasn't been to the boy's grave for a long time so it is possible this could have happened. He drops this thought. He thinks now that he would like to help Clara but doesn't know how. He wonders what he should do and finally asks where the grave was originally. Surprisingly Clara doesn't answer angrily as he had expected but points to the spot near where they are standing by the fountain.

He asks if she is sure of that and she says again in a normal voice that she is. She says she knows it because the grave was right near the fountain and water used to splash on it. He then looks at the figure in the fountain and sees it is that of a little naked boy standing with one of his arms raised and the other one lowered. They are both broken off at the elbow so that it is hard to tell what they looked like originally. He thinks the boy's right hand may have rested on his hip and the left one held his penis which is broken off too. It must have come off with the hand. He figures the fountain probably showed the boy urinating into the bowl below as old fountains sometimes do. This is why he thinks water may have splashed onto Clara's boy's grave—probably when the wind blew that way. In the end again he is sure this is what the fountain was like originally.

The statue's face is also disfigured by time but you can tell it was that of a little boy. He must have looked pretty.

The fountain bowl is dry as was said and there is garbage in it—dried leaves, cigarette butts, and pieces of paper, some of them crumpled up. One of them looks like a whole sheet and has handwriting in purple ink on it. For some reason he feels it is a love letter. He would like to check if this is what it is but feels Clara would disapprove. He doesn't feel brave enough to risk that.

He turns his head back from the bowl and sees Clara is kneeling down on the ground digging at it with a little shovel which she must have brought along in her bag. She is looking for the body of her son. He decides he should help her and kneels down beside her but she is making such good progress he can't see how he could. The shovel delves into the hard soil, scoops it up, throws it to the side, and delves back in again. There is nothing he can do with his bare hands.

Soon something pink emerges from under the gray soil. It is the leg of a plastic doll. Clara digs some more and the outline of the doll's body emerges. Then most of it becomes visible and Clara pulls it out of the ground. It is a plastic doll about a foot long with its left arm and right leg missing. Its head, which turns on its neck, is loose in its socket and is about to fall off. Clara digs more and finds the other leg. She doesn't go on digging looking for the missing arm however. He concludes it isn't there. Although this is a doll he considers it Clara's son's body. He thinks the boy may have died because he lost his left arm.

Clara gets up quickly and puts the doll, its leg, and the shovel in the bag. She then quickly walks over to one of the benches and sits down on it. He follows her. He sits down on her left side feeling sorry he didn't get to help her.

Clara crosses her right leg over her left one and sits like that. Her long white wool coat drapes over her leg. The bag rests in her lap. She is waiting for something. He notices there is a bus stop across from them in the smaller street and wonders if they are waiting for a bus to come for them to take it. He thinks Clara plans to go to some other cemetery to rebury the body of her son there. A big bus just then comes along and stops to pick up or discharge passengers. He isn't sure if there was someone waiting there. The bus drives off without anyone being left behind. He concludes someone must have been waiting there and that he merely hadn't seen the person. He/she must have taken the bus. It apparently was not the bus he and Clara want to take. They are waiting for the right one to come. He prepares himself to wait as long as he has to.

They sit for a while. He gets bored and his eyes roam around through the park. To his surprise he notices there is a piano standing against the wall of the building that abuts the park on the left. It is a small upright badly beaten up with its top missing and ivory gone from some of its keys. A piano stool stands in front of it as if it were still being played on. Although puzzled initially he explains to himself the park must be used for occasional public performances and musicians play on the piano. Just then a figure emerges on his left from the direction they came but on the side of the street the park is on. It is a derelict man in a chewed-up hat, long shabby overcoat, pants too long for him, and worn shoes. He shuffles as he walks along. He makes a turn around the park, circling the fountain, passing them, and then starts another one. This time he walks up to the piano and sits down on the stool with his back to the piano. He throws his right leg over his left one as Clara has done and bundles himself up in his overcoat as if also preparing to wait for a bus. He concludes the man waits for the same number bus as they.

He turns his head right to see if there is a bus coming down the street. There is a lot of traffic in the big street but only passenger cars and trucks and no bus. He keeps on looking. Suddenly to his surprise he hears the sound of music coming from his left. He looks in that direction and sees the derelict man has turned around and is playing the piano. He has taken off his hat and has put it on the corner of the upright part of the piano, has unbuttoned his coat so that its edges are on the ground, and is banging away furiously on the keys. At that instant Clara gets up abruptly as if she has had enough of waiting, walks up to a spot near the fountain, but a different one than where she dug up the doll, gets the shovel out of her bag, squats down, and stars digging in the ground. On this occasion she doesn't kneel down but squats with her knees apart and feet splayed as she had done when showing him the toy piano when they met. This time he realizes it reminds him of a female

155

dog urinating but he doesn't connect it to the first occurrence. He doesn't even remember it.

He doesn't know what she is up to but again wants to help her. Yet before he has time to get up she has dug a shallow hole in the ground, puts the doll and its leg in it, covers them up carelessly with dirt, puts the shovel back into her bag, and stands up. Then she quickly scrapes her feet on the ground a few times as if they were wet or dirty, sending sand and gravel flying backwards in the process, and then takes off at a brisk pace in the direction they came from. While doing this she walks past the man and playfully ruffles the hair on his head with her hand as if they were friends. The man responds in a similar fashion, as if they were friends, by bending his head down and looking up at her from under his brow without stopping to play. Clara doesn't stop but walks on and while moving past the edge of the piano stuffs her bag into its open upright part. Apparently glad to be rid of the bag she moves more energetically after that, swinging her body gaily from side to side, gets onto the sidewalk, and in this manner continues walking in the direction they came from.

His heart sinks. He will lose her! He jumps up and runs after her. The derelict man keeps on playing his bombastic music.

7. circus "laffino"

Not Brahms and Clara in an exit passageway between banks of seats during a performance at a circus which is visiting the town. It is called "Circus Laffino" and is famous for the excellence of its clowns and they were happy to be able to see it. The reason why they are in the exit passageway is because Clara ran out in anger when Not Brahms tried to kiss her on the mouth during a wave of gaiety that overcame the audience in the course of a clown act— a giant, seven-foot female and a three foot male dwarf. The former

156

declared her love for the latter which made him run away, falling into a tub full of water, with her winding up on top of him. Terrified at having offended Clara Not Brahms rushed out after her and caught up with her in the passageway. The passageway dark, illuminated only by the light penetrating from the circus arena. The seats rising some ten rows up on both sides to the height of about fifteen feet. The space under the seats an empty forest of metal struts. The ground below all dug up for some unknown purpose. In one spot close to the passageway half a dozen of big plastic buckets filled with what looks like elephant or horse dung. A couple of shovels lying unconscious on the ground next to them. An appropriate smell emanating from the buckets. Rows upon rows of human behinds visible along the seats in the gaps between the successive rows appropriately accompanying the smell. Metal barriers about four feet high separating the space under the seats from the passageway.

Not Brahms has grabbed Clara by her wrists and is pressing her to the barrier on the right. She is trying to free herself from him, her arms like two metal rods attempting to return to their original form after having been twisted.

Clara (screaming): No! No! No! Let me go!

Her face is a big pale stain darting about in the semidarkness trying to position itself correctly in relation to the two small pale stains of her hands as they dart about in various unexpected directions.

Not Brahms (with despair in his voice at the realization that he is not only in danger of losing Clara but also a hold of her wrists): But Clara, dearest, I didn't have anything bad in mind!

157

Clara *(on the background of loud blaring noises as of giant kazoos or elephants farting coming from the arena):* Yes you did! All you're interested in is taking me to bed!

A wave of laughter from the audience comes streaming into the passageway.

Not Brahms *(despair at being wrongly accused of something he despises replacing the previous despair):* That's not true! I swear! I never even dreamt of that! I truly love you... innocently, purely... like child!

Clara: Bah! *(Her right hand has freed itself from Not Brahms' grip. It flies about like a wasp gone wild as Not Brahms tries to grab it):* You wouldn't even agree to buy our apartment because it didn't suit your financial plans... because you didn't think it was a good deal. Some love.... Innocent....

A regular tsunami wave of laughter from the audience inundates the passageway.

Not Brahms *(turning hot all over from the outrageous accusation, his reason completely gone):* I will buy it! I will buy it on the spot! Right now.... Cash.... I didn't know it mattered so much to you.

He has grabbed Clara's right wrist but the left one has managed to get away and performs a similar wasp-like darting maneuvers.

Clara *(furiously, 100% sure):* No! I don't want it! I wouldn't sell it to you at any price! I will sell it at a loss to someone else!

Not Brahms has managed to grab a hold of Clara's left hand and is in a position he was in before. Clara has put more energy into her body now and is concentrating on it. Not Brahms has noticed it and is pressing Clara with all his might against the barrier. Another set of obscene noises is heard coming from the arena followed by a tsunami wave of laughter from the audience.

Not Brahms *(all sorts of despair mingled in his pleading voice):* But Clara, Clara, please! Be reasonable! I really didn't mean to offend you. I only got carried away by my joy... by the way everyone laughed.... My love just surged up.

Clara *(mobilizing all her force and freeing her body from under Not Brahms'; her wrists stay in his hands however and she remains attached to him by her arms):* No, no, no! You don't love me! All you want is my body! Let go of me! Let go!

A sound of utter bedlam comes from the arena punctuated by thumping noises. A small dark waddling figure appear on the light background of the arena followed by a huge gangly one. They both run down the passageway. The two clowns are making their exit. They run past Not Brahms and Clara, splashing the two with the water with which their clothes are soaked. Their oversize shoes make loud squishing noises. In a couple of seconds they vanish behind the cloth covering the exit.

Not Brahms instinctively follows them with his eyes. As his attention wanders off both of Clara's wrists free themselves from his grip at the same time and she takes off after the clowns. Not Brahms watches with abandonment as she reaches the still swinging cloth at the end of the passageway, stands sharply outlined on the bright background, and is erased by darkness.

The sound from the audience has almost died down.

An early fall mid-morning. The air warm, moist, with particles of mist suspended in it. The distance dissolving in a milky fog. A yard surrounded by low, single-storied brick farm buildings, their tin roofs rusty in places, shiny with moisture. Farm machinery all around—tractors, trailers, plows, harrows, sowing machines, reapers, mechanical hoes, bulldozers—all in bad state of repair, also shiny with moisture, busily rusting. Above the buildings tops of trees protruding, mostly still covered with matted yellow leaves but some with their branches already bare, their tips likewise dissolving in the mist. A smell of wilted leaves like that of cured tobacco mixed with a faint aroma of smoke from burning leaves hanging in the air. Sounds of men's voices mixed with the smells like still another smell coming from an uncertain direction. The ground bare, in places muddy from recent rain. Although not at right angles to each other the buildings form an enclosure, more of a psychological type than physical one, like a pair of hands, their fingers spread, reaching out for something.

Clara in the middle of the yard, walking from one end to the other. She is dressed in a white nurse's pants and blouse outfit with a pair of black pumps on her bare feet. The tops of the shoes scuffed, clumps of earth sticking to the sharp stiletto heels about an inch from the end in a ring like the mark left by wine in an emptied glass. Her blond hair dull, stiff, brittle-looking, badly combed, tied with a narrow crumpled pink band in the back. The face puffy, white, like a lump of dough rolled in flour. The eyes blank, their color nearly gone.

She walks slowly in an unsteady way, reeling at times, as if in shock from some profound trauma, for instance rape. Doesn't seem to know where she is going, nor caring, so long as she is leaving behind what is behind her.

She passes between the last two buildings and finds herself in an open space filled with tall trees. Only the ones up front are fully visible, the farther ones dissolving gradually more and more in the fog. Surprisingly lots of leaves on the ground under the trees like deep yellow puddles, given the amount still left on the branches. The foliage must have been exceptionally thick this year.

Up ahead on her right about a hundred feet away stands a barn of gray weathered wood covered with a rusty tin roof shiny with moisture. The barn has a big door in the wider wall facing to the left and a smaller one in the shorter one which faces Clara. Both are shut. There is a window on the left of the smaller door, its glass dull from the dust gathered on it like fat congealed on top of a pot of soup gone cold.

On seeing the barn Clara becomes energized as if another, vigorous personality had suddenly entered her body. She straightens up, her movements become fluid, pace quickens, face livens up, and gaze grows focused. She stares at the small door and walks toward it. On reaching it she puts her right hand on the handle, presses down on it, pushes forward, opens the door, and steps inside the barn. It is as if she were stepping into her office which she does every day. While moving forward she reaches out with her left hand behind her back and tries to close the door but doesn't quite succeed and leaves it slightly ajar.

The barn is dark inside. In addition to the window on the left of the small door it is illuminated only by another window of the same size which is in the wall on the right, halfway between it and the first of the four horse stalls that extend along that wall all the way to the other end of the barn. There is a horse in the first stall while the other three are empty. A huge old open carriage takes up the free space along the three empty stalls with the big door that was visible from the outside on its left. Like the farm machinery outside

161

it is in bad state of repair and appears not to have been used for a long time. In the corner on the right by the small door there is a pile of hay about six feet high, tightly packed so that its sides go up steeply. A pitchfork lies on the floor in front of it under the window on the right. In the corner on the left there is a pile of oats some three feet high, its cone partly depleted, a shovel stuck into it at a steep angle.

The horse is bay, old, and swaybacked. It is tethered to the trough attached to the wall and is busy eating out of it, as it appears, oats. It sticks its head inside the trough, takes a mouthful of oats, raises its head back up, and munches on what it took in.

Clara pauses briefly on coming in, looks at the horse, walks ahead, and stops, leaning with her back on the pile of hay, facing the horse. She lowers her head and stares at the horse from under her eyebrows.

The horse pays no attention to her, finishes munching, sticks its head inside the trough, takes a mouthful, raises its head, and goes on munching as before.

Clara whistles softly at the horse still looking at it from under her eyebrows.

The horse turns its head toward her, looks, continues munching, then turns its head back and after finishing eating sticks its head back in the trough, takes a mouthful of oats, raises its head, and continues munching.

An expression resembling a smile forms itself on Clara's face. She stands up, cocks her head to one side, sucks in her cheeks, and staring at the horse starts taking off her blouse.

It comes off with some difficulty, leaving her hair more messy than before. Under her blouse Clara's torso is naked, her breasts heavy and sagging, their nipples drawn in from the cold so that they look seriously impaired like hands with all their fingers missing.

Clara tosses her blouse on the floor before her, smooths down her hair with her hands, raises her arms high, and wiggles her torso, whistling softly at the horse again.

This time the horse ignores her however and goes on eating.

Clara moves her torso and arms some more moving away from the pile of hay and performing a dance for the benefit of the horse. She whistles a few more times and this time the horse finally turns its head toward her and looks while busily munching on what is in its mouth.

Clara smiles seductively, moves closer to the horse, kicks off one of her shoes and then the other, and starts humming a melody.

The horse turns its head away from her, makes a deep grunt, and lowers its head into the trough.

Clara isn't discouraged by what has happened however but continues dancing and humming the melody.

The horse continues eating.

Clara seems to have forgotten about it and proceeds with her dance. With her back toward the horse she unbuttons her pants and slowly wiggles her behind out of them. She then turns around, steps with one of her legs out of the pants and then the other, and throws them down on the floor next to the blouse.

163

While this goes on the horse looks once at her but otherwise continues eating.

Clara is wearing pink panties made out of thick material, full, made for comfort rather than looks. She moves continually, writhing her torso and arms and swinging her hips, her feet performing a complicated dance to the rhythm of the melody she is humming.

At one point she puts her hands down on her hips and starts pushing her panties down. Her belly button emerges from under the roll of fabric and then the first strands of her pubic hair. It is surprisingly dark, almost black, and unruly, as if anxious to get out into the open after being confined under the fabric. As she pushes the panties down more, the rest of her pubic hair emerges, dark and thick, the unruly hairs having fallen in with the rest to form one solid bushy shape, to present themselves unified to the world.

Clara pushes her panties down to her ankles, steps out of them first with one leg then with the other, as if out of a puddle of pink paint, picks them up daintily with the tips of her fingers, and drops them on the floor with the rest of her clothes.

She stops humming and stands with her arms raised, her head cocked to one side, her hips to the other, her knees pressed together. The pubic triangle projects itself toward the horse like a bold provocative stare.

The horse pays no attention to Clara however and goes on eating. Clara goes back to humming her melody while moving back to its rhythm toward the stack of hay until her body rests on it. She then raises her right foot, rests it on the hay so as to expose her crotch, and emits a sharp loud whistle.

The horse waits a second or two, phlegmatically lifts its head, and looks with boredom at her while continuing to chew. A gust of wind brings the sound of men's voices through the crack in the door like a faint scent of smoke.

9. *träumerei* 5
(the shark)

Not Brahms is vacationing with Clara on the Baltic Sea. They are on the beach and there is a little boy about four of five years old with them. The boy is Clara's son. Clara is somewhere behind him busy with something and the boy is playing with a little boat in the water. He is dressed in an old-fashioned striped blue and white swimming suit with a top. It has a sailor's collar so that it looks more like a boy's sailor suit than a swimming suit although it is supposed to be the latter. The sea is calm and he can float the boat easily. The boat is actually a sardine can and has a mast in the middle of it with a triangular blue sail attached just on one side that flaps around. The sail actually looks like a flag but is supposed to be a sail and he thinks of it as such.

There is a strong breeze blowing and it blows the boat away from the shore. The boy goes after it and soon is up to his neck in water. He thinks that the boy probably can't swim and yells at him not to go any farther. The boy doesn't listen to him however and soon gets swallowed up by the sea. His head pops up, then goes down, then up and down again—he is about to drown.

He is terrified, yells at the boy, and dives in after him. When he reaches the spot where the boy was, the latter is no longer there. He looks up and sees the boy's head some ten yards ahead of him. The boy seems to be swimming and apparently is going after his boat. He decides to go after the boy—he is sure the latter can't swim well enough and will drown in the end. The boy keeps on swimming however and he has to pursue him.

Eventually there is no sight of the boy and he has forgotten about him. He just keeps on swimming—he has to get somewhere.

The sea gets rough and the waves are big. Swimming gets hard. He is worried he might not make it to where he is going but continues pushing on. Suddenly he feels something bite one of his feet. It must be a shark!

He is terrified and flails away with his arms hoping to swim faster. For a few seconds he feels nothing but then he is bitten again. The shark is going to get him!

He screams and pounds the water with his arms as hard as he can but the shark bites him again. In despair he looks back and sees a wide-open mouth full of sharp teeth and bulging blue eyes in a determined white face sticking out of the water. It isn't a shark but a woman! He is as terrified as before however—being bitten by a woman is as bad as by a shark. But then he notices something familiar in the woman's features. It is Clara! She just doesn't realize it is him she is trying to bite. He has to let her know. He shouts, Clara don't bite! It's me, it's me! She doesn't hear or understand him however and dives down to bite him again.

He lets out a wild scream of despair and wakes up.

10. kafka

There is a knock on the door and Clara's heart sinks. At that very instant she remembers a dream she had during the night in which she was visited by some strange people and she is sure now it is them. It unfolds before her like a film. In the dream she is among

166

black hanging cloths as on a stage and from among similar cloths on the other side of the open space before her step out three tall stately figures all in black with black masks on their faces and walk toward her. They step awkwardly, making loud thumping noises as if wearing platform shoes like actors in classic Greek drama and move toward her. They have business to do with her. The character in the middle, the tallest of the three who wears a big gold crown on his head, carries a golden object in his hands carefully in front of him as something precious. They come up to her and stop. The main character steps forward and raises the object in his hands so that it is on the level of his chest and directly below her eyes. She sees it is a gold crown, smaller than the one he is wearing but beautiful, studded with rubies, emeralds, sapphires, and diamonds. She has never seen anything so beautiful before. The man raises the crown higher and forward— he wants to place it on her head. She is overcome with joy. The crown is for her! She knew it was a crown the moment she saw it and knew it was for her and she has been waiting for it all her life knowing it would eventually come. She bends her head down and feels the crown being placed on top of it. It is a little tight and hurts her skull but that doesn't matter. She isn't used to it, that is all. With time she won't feel it. She lifts her head and looks into the man's eyes. They are empty black holes in the mask and there is nothing inside them. The sight frightens her but she remembers the crown and feels gratitude for the man. He raises his right hand and she knows it is for her to place her left one in it. She does that, the man turns left, she follows him, and they all walk in the direction the men came from. She feels the heavy thumping of their feet on the floor and observes how barely audible and delicate her footsteps are in comparison. She thinks this might bother her but is pleased to notice that it doesn't and so she pushes the thought out of her mind. She has gotten used to the pressure of the crown on her head and likes to feel her hand being supported by the man's. They reach the black cloths on the other side of the stage—open space—and step behind them. It is totally dark there, all of a sudden the men are gone, and she finds herself alone in a busy street with lots of people and traffic. She looks around as if to get a bearing or for a taxi. She has forgotten about the crown and doesn't seem to feel it.

The knocking is repeated and Clara doesn't have time to think more about the dream. She isn't sure if it dissipates at this point or goes on. She rushes to the door.

With her heart in her throat she opens it and sees two men standing on the landing before her. The first man is short with dirty blond hair and small round steel-rimmed glasses and is dressed in a suit made out of a thick grayish-green wool material with a short tight-fitting jacket and wide pants as if made over from a military uniform. The second man stands directly behind the first and all Clara can see is his head with straight black hair that falls over his forehead like an injured wing of a crow and a long bony face. When she opens the door he is looking sideways to his right and is sucking vigorously on a cigarette which he holds in his fingers like on a straw in a glass. She pays no attention to how he is dressed now or after that.

The first man says his name is Marcel and that they represent the *Karl Marx Stadt Staatstheater* (State Theater of Karl Marx Stadt, the city formerly known as Chemnitz in the German Democratic Republic or GDR). Could they have a minute of her time?

Clara's heart has pushed its way inside her head between her ears and is thumping so loudly she is afraid she will miss what the man is saying. The dream is coming true! She composes herself however—she has to rise to the occasion for another opportunity like this isn't likely to come soon—and answers that of course they can. Would they like to step in?

They would gladly, the first man says, the two men step into the hallway, and Clara shuts the door.

She is in the process of making her morning coffee and the coffee pot is making complaining noises on the kitchen stove about having been forgotten, so she has to attend to it. Would they mind coming into the kitchen with her?

They would gladly, the first man says exactly as just a moment ago and the three go into the kitchen. The coffee pot simmers down as soon as they all come into the kitchen, as if pacified by Clara's presence, although it must have been just an unrelated momentary buildup of steam in the pot. The coffee isn't quite ready and Clara leaves the pot alone. She stays near the stove however in order to attend to it when it is time. The men have stopped by the table in the middle of the kitchen.

Would they like to sit down? And would they like to have some coffee when it is ready?

With gratitude, the first man says, and the two make themselves comfortable on the chairs, the first man facing the stove and the second one on the side on the first man's right. He still hasn't said a word and is intimately involved with his cigarette. He must be from the *Stasi* (*Staatssicherheit*, the GDR Secret Police), Clara thinks, a "guardian angel" who is to make sure the man Marcel doesn't misbehave. The ashes on the tip of his cigarette have grown long and will fall to the floor any second. She gets one of the saucers from the counter and puts it down on the table in front of the man.

Would he mind using it? She and her husband don't smoke and there isn't an ashtray in the house.

The man grunts, tosses his head to move the hair off his forehead, shakes the ashes off the tip of the cigarette into the saucer with one forceful tap of his finger, and goes back to sucking on the cigarette.

He seems to be part horse, Clara observes not only without the least sign of contempt for the man but perhaps even with a trace of admiration. Horses are not known for being oversentimental and that's what she likes in people. She goes back to the counter, gets three cups and saucers, and sets them up next to the stove.

They would like to come to the purpose of their visit, the first man says.

Yes, she is listening, Clara replies, the pressure inside her head building up again after having subsided.

The *Staatstheater* would like to offer her a role in a production they are undertaking. Would she be interested in it?

She might... would.... Depending on the nature of the production.

Her heart is up between her ears again and she can barely hear the man speak. The hoped-for moment has arrived.

It is a stage production although it might be turned into a film.

A tragedy?... Greek? Clara blurts out, the nature of the production being of little importance to her at this instant. The figures in the dream must have been from a classical Greek play.

Well... a tragedy, yes... and part Greek perhaps... influenced by Greek tragedy for sure.

Clara's heart makes a sound of joy like a nightingale. She relaxes finally. Her dream has come true. She listens calmly to what the man says.

It is a modern work, an adaptation of Kafka's "In the Penal Colony."

Clara has heard of Kafka of course but doesn't know the short story. She thinks it is a novel. The prospect is very exciting, perhaps even more than a classical Greek play would be.

She finds the idea exciting, she says. What would be her role in the production?

That of the wife of the commander of the colony, the first man replies. As she knows, the character doesn't appear in the work but it has been added.

It is a tragic figure though....

Tragic?... Yes. She is tragic.

Like Medea, Electra, or Clytemnestra?

The man hesitates for a moment. More like Clytemnestra.... She prepares the food that the convict consumes during the execution. Does she remember the story?

Vaguely, Clara replies, blushing. She convinces herself she might have read it a long time ago and has forgotten it.

Well, in the work, the food is always the same—some sort of sweet porridge which is supposed to assuage the victim's suffering. But in the adaptation the food varies depending on the victim. It might

171

be sweet and tasty but it might be horribly bad. The victim still would eat it. Kafka says that the victim always eats the porridge because it tastes good. The pleasure of eating masks the pain. In their production though they show that the victim eats the food even when it tastes bad, when it contributes to the victim's suffering. It is the instinctive need to eat that is activated by the torture. The victim eats even though the food brings him more pain. He has been turned by the suffering into an animal. And he understands that and suffers because of this even more.

So she, Clara says, that is the character in the production, comes up with different recipes for the victims to increase their suffering... depending on their crime.

That is correct, the man replies, smiling.

Clara is very excited. Her nervousness is all gone now and her imagination is racing.

That is very interesting, she says. Might she come up with her own recipes?

Of course, the man replies. That would be wonderful. It wasn't planned like that but it would be welcome. An actor's active participation in the development of a production is always welcome as it improves the work, makes it more natural, organic.

Did he say in the book (she still thinks the work is a novel) the victim eats a sweet porridge?... Like a rice pudding with milk and raisins?

Yes, the man replies, something like that.

Well, you might mix it with sardines, lots of sardines and oil... castor oil.

That's wonderful, great, the first man laughs. She has great talent in this area. She might find a job elsewhere after the production is over. With the *Stasi* for instance. They need talent like that.

Clara and the first man laugh. The second man snorts, tossing his head again and freeing his forehead from the annoying hair. He has finished the original cigarette and has started on a new one without Clara's having noticed when.

He is a centaur, Clara thinks, the topic of Greek tragedy having evoked in her this association. (Her interest in him has grown and in her excitement she has failed to observe she is faced with a situation opposite to the original Greek—it is the man's head that is horse's and the lower part of his body human.) Did centaurs copulate with women in old Greek myths? She muses on. Did they beget children? And what were the children then—human or centaurs?... Or perhaps horses?... She wonders if she will get to know the man better when she takes the job. She wouldn't mind at all it if she did.

There are loud impatient noises coming from the pot. This time the coffee is ready. Clara interrupts her thoughts and turns away to pour it into the cups.

11. the ball

There were three bands playing on four floors. No band played on the third floor and dancers followed the music from the floor above and below whichever was more audible at a particular moment. Some people sang their own songs as they danced which proved to be the wisest strategy.

Darkness was the operational word everywhere. An occasional impromptu source of light or its reflection on a table or wall provided enough guidance so that the ball was able to proceed. The music stand lights, although shielded from the public, contributed also in a measurable way to the ball's success. The effect of all of this was to turn persons into their own profiles—a nose sticking out dangerously like a long triangular knife or a little turned-up button sewed onto the face of a rag doll, a chin jutting out like a ledge on a wall for holding something or a receding one resembling an ice cube nearly dissolved in warm water, a triangle of lank hair like a ripped-off jacket lapel hanging lose or a woman's coiffure like a bouquet of exuberant roses incongruously protruding out of the top of a skull. Some people had holes in their chests as in a surrealist painting. This was often due to a glass being clutched close to the chest while dancing. Drinks (free) were served in tall glasses consisting of blue phosphorescent liquid, which flickered like lights on graves, extremely sweet but with a bitter aftertaste suggesting that of pulverized burnt human bones. It was liberally laced with alcohol which acted in the predictable fashion—often quickly and with visible effect.

Conversations sparkled, drinks splashed, and partners would regularly be changed unwittingly in the middle of a dance.

Clara's long black dress and Spanish shawl *(mantilla)* of the same color fitted well into the surroundings. A cat finds itself a comfortable place among pillows on the sofa the same way. She came with a party of about a dozen people—acquaintances rather than friends—who occupied a big round table but because of the darkness and natural human propensity for exploring new places and friendships soon found herself among strangers. Occasionally in the tenebrous air two or three members of the original gang would surface around her and she wasn't sure if they had been

174

with her all along, for a while, or had merely coalesced in her vicinity at that instant.

While finding herself once amidst an unusually high number of the members of the original gang—six or seven out of the original eleven, twelve, or thirteen—sitting together at a table she wound up talking to a man who may have been a friend or acquaintance of one or more of her companions but whom she had not met before. She couldn't see his features in the darkness but found herself attracted almost physically to him like a small iron object to a powerful magnet due to his huge size and overbearing personality. He must have been in the finance business for he was good with numbers the way some people are good with words. This added to his attractiveness in her eyes. In the near total darkness he seemed to shine with physical glamour. What an amazing man, she thought from time to time as they danced, her consciousness coming to the surface for a brief instant like the head of a drowning person bobbing up from under the water in which he or she is drowning. How wonderful that I have met him. I have been waiting for someone like him—him specifically—all my life.

When at one point he asked if she wanted to go to the kitchen, knowing precisely what he meant although he explained neither the word "kitchen" nor the purpose of their going there, she agreed readily with a laughter-laced "Yes."

"The kitchen" was exactly what the words implied—a big room with stainless-steel stoves, sinks, a table in the center, and three enormous refrigerators almost as big as the room itself so that it seemed to be one of them, perhaps the smallest one at that. It was lugubriously illuminated by a row of leukemic neon lights running the length of the ceiling. Something must have been wrong with the electrical circuit they were on for they flickered feebly, about to go out like fishes in their final throes tossed out onto sand.

She knew what he would do and resigned herself to it but was overwhelmed by the actual act and would have backed out if she could have at the last moment. He lifted her up like a child—a doll—in the air, pressed her against the edge of one of the refrigerators, with one gesture of his powerful hand raised her skirt above her waist, in an instant produced an eager, ready, and giant penis, and, as if her underwear were not there, was inside her.

She laughed to minimize the importance of what had happened and said something to the effect, did he realize what he was doing? but this had no effect on his actions. He ignored her words and went about his business as if they had no relevance to what was happening. He held her up in the air all the time without the least sign of effort as she could tell by his easy and relaxed breathing, which she found impressive.

His pleasure was genuine, she could tell, and so was hers, which frightened her, and she began to protest more, all the time trying to turn what was happening into a joke. Then he was finished and she felt herself peaking too and couldn't hold back a series of hoarse screams that came throbbing out of her throat.

When he put her down she was shocked at what had happened but suddenly got an idea which she thought would remedy the situation and said perversely, You see, you didn't get in after all.

He laughed, zipping up his pants and said, It was a great pleasure staying outside.

Continuing in this fashion would have been just right for her but at that instant he turned around and without saying a word walked out the door, his back a fourth huge stainless-steel refrigerator.

She was aghast. What was she to do? Unsteady, reeling, like a moth flying to a light, she walked to the black rectangle of the door and after blindly wending her way through the dark maze of walkways found herself in the cavernous dance hall.

Lights were thawing out here and there along the walls, drinks gave off blue flashes in the tall clenched glasses, and profiles of people moved to the existent/nonexistent music, some of them with surrealist holes in their chests.

12. after the ball(ing)

Gone berserk with claustrophobia the train dashed madly down the tunnels trying to get out, taking first this, then that, and then still another one, its body hitting now one, now the other wall, scarping them, making a racket like thousands of doors being slammed in great anger at nearly the same time or shaken in desperation in an attempt to open them, shaking as if it were a door it itself was trying to open, pulling and pushing exasperatedly on its handle. The air, black from the speed, rushed in through the open windows high up under the ceiling wrapping itself around the faces of the passengers, few at this hour, stifling them so that they pulled with their hands on its currents as on black veils trying to free their gasping mouths in order to breathe, their eyes bulging, white around the irises, with small dark dots in the middle. The gaze of some of them rolled on the ground like empty beer bottles at times finding a permanent resting place in dark corners under the long varnished wooden benches running the lengths of the cars.

177

Clara sat on one of these alone, at times seeming the only one in the car, her feet tightly pressed together, knees the same, sticking up under the long black dress like the prognathous jaw of a person, elbows dug into her sides as if escorting a reluctant herself to where the train was taking her, the fringed black *mantilla*-shawl draped over her head and covering her torso, converting her into a Spanish widow or a chaperone-*dueña* of herself, her face puffy with silence, swollen, flabby, trembling to the rhythm of the shaking like water in a bowl, flabby to this degree for the first time in her life, it having crossed over the threshold between middle age and old that very night, embarking on the short straight road that leads to decrepitude, the chin heavier than a few hours earlier, flesh sagging along the lower jaw line like wax growing soft, the nose longer, the eyes bleary, unfocused, their irises faded like washed denim. In her mind there was only the memory of the kitchen she'd been to with the man or rather the image of the three huge refrigerators that stood there as if she'd taken them along with her and there was no room in it for anything else. She also felt along her spine the pressure of the edge of the one the man had pressed her against as if it'd come off the refrigerator together with her and had stayed painfully attached to her, dug into her flesh. Of the man she recalled only his enormous strength and overwhelming personality and the shiny serrated edges of his wingtip shoes which she couldn't take her eyes off during the event, frightening like the whites of the bulging eyes of an attacking dog.

At one point her eyes focused on her shoes whose tips were timidly sticking out from under the hem of her dress and she noticed a round wet spot on the left one. It looked clear like water and for an instant she thought it was a tear that had dropped from her eye unbeknownst to herself (she didn't remember crying) but concluded it was probably the man's semen that had either dropped directly from him or perhaps from her; she seemed to feel she had read somewhere or knew from experience that semen becomes clear after being exposed to air.

The semen and the memory it evoked brought on in her a feeling of revulsion but she was too weak to move her eyes away from the spot or to close them and so she resigned herself to being tortured by it for as long as it wanted.

At one point unexpectedly a pale dot appeared at the end of the tunnel and the train realized it had finally found its way from under the ground. It stopped rattling and shaking and trying to devote every ounce of energy to its goal ran in as straight a line as possible toward it and in a matter of seconds found itself out in the open.

A huge river lay before it filled like a big peasant bed with tousled bedclothes with milky water, mist, and vague outlines of islands with sandy beaches overgrown with willow trees and osiers. There was a station right on the bank up ahead and the train slowed down gradually and came to a stop. The doors in the cars on the right opened in unison followed instantly by some meaningless sounds made by a male voice on the loudspeaker which rushed outside all together and disappeared there like bats or birds finding an opening after having been held in confinement for a long time.

Mechanically, as if ordered to do it, Clara got up, walked out onto the platform, turned right, and proceeded to walk in the direction the train came from. The world lay hidden in the mist separated from her by a row of tall black bars of an iron fence. Somehow she found her way out from behind it, came to a broad highway that ran parallel to the river, crossed it without stopping (there was no traffic in it in either direction), and like a moth flying blindly toward a light pushed on toward the darkness among the bushes and

179

under the trees growing on the slope of the ridge that stretched along the river.

Her feet found a paved path leading up the ridge and she followed it still blindly first going to the right, then left, then right and left again, and so on, climbing all the time the steep slope. She reached the top of the ridge without stopping, crossed the wide avenue that ran along it parallel to the highway on the bottom, and once again crossed it without stopping because in it there was also no traffic in either direction. She got up onto the sidewalk on the other side (it was paved with gray hexagonal tiles, she observed) and collapsed under a hedge that separated the sidewalk from the grounds of hotels and fancy high-rises that stretched in a row along the street as far as the eye could see to the right and left.

There the street sweepers found her a few hours later and swept her up with their wide stiff brushes together with withered leaves, discarded bouquets of wilted flowers, crumpled love letters, and other street debris from which she was no longer distinguishable.

13. end of the line/end of the affair

He had spent nearly twenty-four hours (twenty-two and a quarter, from eight-thirty the night before to quarter to seven in the evening the following day) cooped up alone in the close sleeping car compartment which should have been unbearable but proved delightfully refreshing as if spent in the company of a person he couldn't get enough of but actually was only he himself. The train left the station without making a sound as if trying to sneak out unnoticed and in a matter of minutes was out in the suburbs among single storied factories and warehouses interspersed with vacant lots having followed byways and shortcuts he didn't know existed and then unexpectedly there was nothing but open country all around with the fields empty, already harvested or left fallow from the preceding year, and the light rapidly fading as if progressively being left behind. Huge square bottomless holes a quarter of a mile on each side would appear from time to time next to the railroad tracks surrounded by rows of slender trees (poplars?) planted close together which were freshly plowed fields in reality with the incredibly rich black soil (reputedly as many as seven feet deep) brought up to the surface and exposed to the spectator's eye. Then came the night with the world whooshing like black wind past the partly open window The wind itself resting like a cold and heavy bundle of freshly mowed grass somebody threw on top of him as he lay stretched out on his back on the hard narrow bed. The smell of sage, wormwood, thyme, peppermint. The golden straws of stars way up in the black firmament when he wiggled his head back on the pillow and craned his eyes toward the window. Only three stations during the night, small and empty at that. The morning cool and fresh with the flat land running frantically next to the train, managing to keep up. The air gradually heating up, finally turning the compartment into an oven, the narrow varnished slats of yellow wood on the walls like iron bars heated up to that degree. But the exhilaration at being alone undiminished. The dialog with himself going on and on. Only another three or four stations during most of the day, each a small white stucco-covered cube in the middle of nowhere, with no settlement as far as the eye could see on the flat landscape, although huge open-air markets spread out on both sides of the tracks like camps of war refugees or victims of a major natural disaster. Wares in stalls but also laid out on the ground on top of blankets. Mostly housewares—pots and pans, buckets, iron and plastic, washboards, brushes, brooms, but also food and toys, a surprising number of toys, most surprising among them giant pink teddy bears which no one bought. He bought bottled water at all three of the stations and at the last one in addition a watermelon—white- and green-striped, small and round like a child's head, which the woman sliced up for him right in her hand with a huge triangular knife. It was blood-red inside and cool, its juice sweet like syrup. Toward the evening the air began to cool off, announcing the proximity of the sea. Stations began popping up like people jumping to their feet to wave down the train. Passengers got off in droves at them so that it began to scare him—he will be left alone in the end to live through the impending, inevitable disastrous crash. He held firm however and was the only one to get off at his station which was the end of the line.

After a few seconds, without a whistle, the train started up again and chugged along to where a huge square white board with a solid red circle in the middle and a bunch of black concentric ones superimposed on the latter as on a target practice board blocked its way about a hundred yards down and then headed backwards, immediately veering off to its left along the tracks that were not visible from where he stood. Then suddenly it was gone, disappearing behind the curvature of the earth and the mist which like a huge frosted glass bell covered the landscape. Now he was truly alone.

His back was turned to where the train vanished. The suitcase that he had put down on the ground pressed against his left leg like a frightened dog. The ground was crunchy under his feet, a mixture of sand and pulverized gray stone that looked like cement. Some ten feet ahead a narrow paved road ran parallel to the railroad tracks continuing beyond the sign that blocked their way and disappearing in the mist not far beyond it. On the far side it was accompanied by sparsely spaced stubby wooden poles on which wires hung limply reflecting the laziness of the crew that had strung them. Another road, unpaved, more a footpath that a road, ran perpendicularly from this road from about where he stood, curving all the time to the right until disappearing some two hundred feet away behind a low narrow and long structure built from cinder blocks and painted white, with a flat tarred roof. A few wires branched off from one of the poles and ran toward the building merging somewhere with it. There were no doors or windows visible in the building, all of them being apparently on the other side, facing the sea.

The latter lay about another hundred feet away dull gray and still, barely distinguishable from the flat gray beach, with only an occasional tiny wave breaking along its edge, white like the inside of the eyelid of person suffering from anemia. A white frilly garland stretching along the beach a few feet away from where the waves broke marked its limit—plastic bags, bottles, paper, condoms, and other kind of debris deposited there by high tide. The line where the sea and the air merged in the distance was blurred by the mist so that it was impossible to find it.

Not Brahms breathed easier. He had arrived! The structure before him was the motel that had been recommended to him, which he had contacted and where he was going to spend the next two weeks.

He looked forward to lying for hours on end on the hard damp beach under a leaden sky, fully dressed or in his beach robe, his towel damp and scrunched up under him, the sand under the towel having arranged itself into hard ridges like those on a washboard, digging itself into his flesh and bones, the cold wet air streaming out of the water a few feet away from his feet like from a dank cellar, a strong smell of salt and iodine stuffed like wads of cotton in his nostrils, to wading also for hours on end in the calf-high water, ice-cold, hurting the bones of his feet as if trying to break them, the bottom flat, concrete-hard, with sharp ridges in it formed by currents which also hurt his feet as he stumbled or stubbed his toes on them at times hundreds of yards away from the shore, the mist like a huge glass bell over him obscuring everything, earth and water, water and sky, up and down, so that he didn't know which way to go, to conversely squirming on the cramped incomprehensibly shrunk rectangle of his towel with the sun directing all its heat at him, sweat pouring out of him, standing out in beads like lymph on a skinned spot on one's body, desiccating like a jelly fish tossed out on the beach, to afternoons spent on the hard narrow bunk bed in his room in a hundred degree heat, the bare cinderblock walls painted a shiny pale turquoise wet with moisture, the sweat on his body trying to match, matching, overmatching the moisture on the walls, the coarse wooden furniture—bunk bed, table, chair—shiny with the dark, tea-colored varnish, out of place like someone else's pulled teeth placed in a toothless person's mouth, the tall narrow opening covered with a thin flowered plastic indicating the closet, a not much wider opening of the same height behind the same thin flowery plastic indicating the bathroom, the latter's walls the same as in the room, the toilet bowl in the corner without a seat, the sink stuck crooked to one of the walls, the shower head bending down tired from the opposite wall over a round hole in the concrete floor for a drain, to pitch-dark nights with dreamless stretches of sleep as if training runs for death, to hours of wakefulness between the stretches of sleep with the only awareness the sheen of the darkness like wet black paint on everything, to breakfasts of scalding hot straw-colored tea tasting of aluminum from the aluminum pot it was steeped in with gooey clay-like rye bread served with sickeningly sweet beet jam, to lunches of oats porridge served with cucumber and tomato salad the latter tasteless and crunchy like glass, with tiny cured black olives like goat droppings in it, to dinners of the same oats porridge accompanying undercooked chicken cut up into pieces, all skin and bones, with hardly any meat, a product of poultry concentration camps.

Yuriy Tarnawsky has authored some three dozen books of fiction, poetry, drama, essays, and translations in Ukrainian and English, including three volumes of interrelated mininovels (his own genre) *The Placebo Effect Trilogy,* the novel *Warm Arctic Nights*, and a volume of heuristic poetry *Modus Tollens.* His affinity for animals is well exemplified not only in *Crocodile Smiles* but also in such books as the collection of stories *Short Tails*, the second volume of the *Trilogy*, *The Future of Giraffes*, the novel *The Iguanas of Heat,* and most vividly in his best-known novel *Three Blondes and Death*. He was born in Ukraine but was raised and educated in the West. An engineer and linguist by training, he has worked as computer scientist specializing in Artificial Intelligence at IBM Corporation as well as Professor of Ukrainian Literature and Culture at Columbia University. He lives with his wife Karina in the New York City metropolitan area.

A Checklist of JEF Titles

- [ ] 0   *Projections* by Eckhard Gerdes
- [ ] 2   *Ring in a River* by Eckhard Gerdes
- [ ] 3   *The Darkness Starts Up Where You Stand* by Arthur Winfield Knight
- [ ] 4   *Belighted Fiction*
- [ ] 5   *Othello Blues* by Harold Jaffe
- [ ] 9   *Recto & Verso: A Work of Asemism and Pareidolia* by Dominic Ward & Eckhard Gerdes (Fridge Magnet Edition)
- [ ] 9B   *Recto & Verso: A Work of Asemism and Pareidolia* by Dominic Ward & Eckhard Gerdes (Trade Edition)
- [ ] 11   *Sore Eel Cheese* by The Flakxus Group (Limited Edition of 25)
- [ ] 14   *Writing Pictures: Case Studies in Photographic Criticism 1983-2012* by James R. Hugunin
- [ ] 15   *Wreck and Ruin: Photography, Temporality, and World (Dis)order* by James R. Hugunin
- [ ] 17   *John Barth, Bearded Bards & Splitting Hairs*
- [ ] 18   *99 Waves* by Persis Gerdes
- [ ] 23   *The Laugh that Laughs at the Laugh: Writing from and about the Pen Man, Raymond Federman*
- [ ] 24   *A-Way with it!: Contemporary Innovative Fiction*
- [ ] 28   *Paris 60* by Harold Jaffe
- [ ] 29   *The Literary Terrorism of Harold Jaffe*
- [ ] 33   *Apostrophe/Parenthesis* by Frederick Mark Kramer
- [ ] 34   *Journal of Experimental Fiction 34: Foremost Fiction: A Report from the Front Lines*
- [ ] 35   *Journal of Experimental Fiction 35*
- [ ] 36   *Scuff Mud* (cd)
- [ ] 37   *Bizarro Fiction: Journal of Experimental Fiction 37*
- [ ] 38   *ATTOHO #1* (cd-r)
- [ ] 39   *Journal of Experimental Fiction 39*
- [ ] 40   *Ambiguity* by Frederick Mark Kramer
- [ ] 41   *Prism and Graded Monotony* by Dominic Ward
- [ ] 42   *Short Tails* by Yuriy Tarnawsky
- [ ] 43   *Something Is Crook in Middlebrook* by James R. Hugunin
- [ ] 44   *Xanthous Mermaid Mechanics* by Brion Poloncic
- [ ] 45   *OD: Docufictions* by Harold Jaffe
- [ ] 46   *How to Break Article Noun* by Carolyn Chun*
- [ ] 47   *Collected Stort Shories* by Eric Belgum
- [ ] 48   *What Is Art?* by Norman Conquest
- [ ] 49   *Don't Sing Aloha When I Go* by Robert Casella
- [ ] 50   *Journal of Experimental Fiction 50*
- [ ] 51   *Oppression for the Heaven of It* by Moore Bowen*
- [ ] 52   *Elder Physics* by James R. Hugunin

JEF
Journal of Experimental Fiction

* Winners of the Kenneth Patchen Award for the Innovative Novel